SILVER SERIES

SUPERB WRITING
TO FIRE THE IMAGINATION

Meredith Hooper writes, 'Growing up on the southern edge of the dry brown continent of Australia I always knew that the white frozen continent of Antarctica lay beyond, on the other side of the ocean, the next shore to the one I stood on.

'I wanted to travel to Antarctica. I never thought I would. I read about it, and wrote about it. Then, the Australian Antarctic Division selected me to go to Antarctica to research this novel in 1994. Since then, I've been back to live on an American scientific base, and to spend time on the Royal Navy's ice patrol vessel, *HMS Endurance*. *The Pole-seekers* draws deeply on my experiences of Antarctica, and on researching the accounts of earlier explorers.'

Meredith Hooper has been awarded the Antarctica Service Medal by the National Science Foundation, on behalf of the United States Congress. *The Journal of Watkin Stench*, the companion novel to *The Pole-seekers*, was shortlisted for the Carnegie Medal.

The Pole-seekers

Meredith Hooper

Illustrated by Trevor Newton

Hodder
Children's
Books

A division of Hodder Headline Limited

A Catalogue record for this book is available from
the British Library

ISBN 0 340 75734 5

Typeset by Avon Dataset Ltd, Bidford-on-Avon, Warks

Printed and bound in Great Britain by
The Guernsey Press Co. Ltd, Channel Islands

Hodder Children's Books
A Division of Hodder Headline Limited
338 Euston Road
London NW1 3BH

Hackle and Meredith Hooper dedicate this book to
their families left behind in London
when they travelled south to the Unknown Land.

Acknowledgement

I would like to thank the Australian Antarctic Division
for selecting me to travel to Antarctica with the
Australian National Antarctic Research Expeditions to
research *The Pole-seekers*. I am truly grateful – M.H.

ONE

There was something strange about the rat. He was one of us. But his fur was different. We ships' rats are proud of our fur. It's smooth, soft, dark. But this rat's fur was two times thicker, two times longer, than any rat I'd ever seen. It hunched around his shoulders like a second coat. Except that this was summer, and hot, and he didn't need all that fur.

'Where's he *from*, Hackle?' whispered Eddie.

'Somewhere we don't know about,' I muttered. 'But I reckon he's come off the black ship.'

We'd been lurking around the Dock watching the black ship for days. Peculiar things were going on board. The Hefties – that's what we call the humans who travel on ships, FTs, Fellow Travellers – were sweating as they heaved the stuff into the holds. But what interested us most was the food. Boxes and barrels and sacks of it, too much even for greedy Hefties. Mountains of meat. Enough flour to keep a baker's shop going for years. Tins full of I don't know what, and more grog than you'd dare dream about. And the chocolate! We'd already sampled some, and it was mouth-dribbling good.

We each knew what the other was thinking. This was the ship for us. Who cared where it was going when there was so much to eat on board.

But we had to wait for our orders. We go where our Leader tells us. Beyond the heavy Dock gates the river swirled past, strong brown water carrying barges and rowing-boats, dead dogs and drowned logs. Ships moved down the river on every tide towards the sea, setting out on new journeys, bound for distant ports. On board every ship, occupying the spaces that belonged to them by right, were the ships' rats. We had our comfortable homes on shore, of course. But ships were where we belonged. Travel and adventure – that's what we lived for. Especially us young rats.

We watched the strange rat with the thick fur sniffing around the crates piled on the dock side. He seemed to be checking for something.

'Let's follow him,' I whispered. 'Let's find out what he's here for.'

Suddenly I was dangling in the air, my feet scrabbling. A Guard Rat with a mean face had me by the back of my neck. Eddie was pinned under his foot.

'You two are doing a lot of snooping,' he said. 'Scram!'

TWO

Eddie and I scuttled to the warehouse at the back of the Dock and crouched on a high shelf. The warehouse was a safe and favourite place. Rich smells of cinnamon and coriander stored in the dim coolness drifted around us, and we dreamed of faraway places.

My cousin Archie Stench came panting up.

'You've been Summoned!' Archie gasped out, and stood staring, awkwardly.

Summoned! None of us young rats ever received a Summons. We got rid of Archie, we didn't want him watching us. Then we worried. What if the Guard Rat had reported us – but we weren't doing anything really wrong.

We had to be outside the main gates of the Naval Wharf just before midnight. A Guide Rat would take us to the Meeting Place.

The night was hot and still with a full moon. That made travelling dangerous. We went the safest route, along the rubbish-rich muddy bank of the small river which looped into the great river just beyond the Dock. The Naval Wharf filled the angle where river met river. It was out of bounds to us young rats and we didn't break those kind of rules. The Navy gave many of us our livelihood – ships to sail in, food to eat, good places to live on shore; but we all treated the Navy with respect.

The Guide Rat was waiting. He checked our names, then we were in. Rats slipped silently like tight black shadows between the buildings. 'Now,' said our Guide. We dropped down a grating, up into a storeroom, dodging between bulky iron chains and coiled ropes, and through a door. Our Guide began climbing a narrow spiral staircase. My heart tightened. We meet in secret places, in cellars, behind walls, where we can't be seen, with escape routes planned. Our routes are life and death to us. Stairs are dangerous.

But up we had to climb. At the top we stepped into a small high room, its round walls made completely of glass. Moonlight flooded onto a floor seething with rats. Eddie and I scrambled up to the narrow window ledge. Outside, the great river flowed past, wide and silver. Distant lights winked on the far bank. I shivered with the excitement, and the power of the water.

A group of Seniors stood on a table surrounding our

Leader, Blackwall. Blackwall! His long thin snout scarred by battles, a Leader to be proud of. He raised his arm.

'We begin as always by singing The Ships' Rat Song.'

The words of the stirring song rang through the room.

We are the ships' rats. Ships' rats are we.
Bold and strong, fearless and free.
Travelling far over ocean and sea.
Working together!
Ships' rats forever!

Now the singing deepened, with a drum-like, menacing beat.

We are the ships' rats. Ships' rats are we.
Cunning and cautious, watchful and free.
United against our great enemy.
Fighting together!
Ships' rats forever!

We thumped our tails, and raised clenched claws in the air.

'Enough!' Blackwall's voice cut through the noise. 'Welcome, each of you, to the Navy's Experimental Lighthouse. Your safety here is assured.' He glanced towards the stairs. 'The Navy never carries out experiments on the night of a full moon. But – as always – we must be cautious. Our enemies' agents are everywhere.

'You know the terrible facts. The brown rats have driven us from our rightful territories. They have conquered the land that is ours. But we ships' rats still

possess the ports! And the ships that sail from the ports
are ours – as long as we are vigilant.'

We cheered. But Blackwall's tail was lashing, whiplike.

'The battle, as you know, has spread beyond the seas.
Our enemies attack us in lands that have always belonged
to us, that are ours by right, or by discovery. We are
fighting for our territory. We are fighting for our lives.'

A shiver passed through us. Some hissed, some snarled.

Blackwall smiled grimly. 'Now news has come.
Important news for all of us ships' rats. I call on our
honoured visitor. Pedro.'

As if out of nowhere, the strange rat we'd seen at the
Dock stepped forward, wearing his thick fur like a
badge of otherness. He stared at us, but it was as if he
saw behind our eyes. Then he gazed away, through the

windows, at the sky-sailing moon. Every one of us in that small round room by the great river, was silent, waiting.

'We all remember tales told by our grandfathers of a Land far to the South. Mysterious, uncertain, a Land of shifting rumours, beyond imagining.'

His voice was deep, clear.

'To us here in the North the South means hot days. The sweet smells of tropical nights. Surf curling on to sandy beaches, good times.

'But go further south. Then further south again. Dip down the curve of our great Earth. Reach towards the furthest south. There, beyond all else, lies a great Unknown Land. Hidden. Waiting. Buried in deep ice, shrouded in glittering snow. Colder than frozen iron.

'I have been there. I have seen it. I accompanied a small band of Hefties and together we lived ashore one long dark winter. When summer came the Hefties explored. Then they left. I bear the evidence of my journey about me. The length and thickness of my fur, grown in defence against the bitter cold.

'This is my proof.'

He stared at us again, with sharp dark eyes.

'My journey was brief. I saw little. But of one thing I am certain. The Unknown Land is still unknown. Our enemies the brown rats have not got there. Yet.

'Can we ships' rats conquer and hold the Unknown Land for ourselves? Can *we* get there first – carve out our homes, establish our rights, ahead of our enemies? We do not know. Because we have not tried.

'Now our chance has come. A ship is preparing to depart for the Unknown Land. It is here, in our Dock. I have checked the supplies. I have studied the Hefties. I know the signs. Guard Rats patrol the area watching for spying eyes. Our enemies must discover nothing.'

'The black ship!' hissed Eddie.

Blackwall stepped forward.

'The Seniors have met. We have decided. We will send an Advance Expedition to the Far South. We need to gather vital information before further decisions and commitments are made.

'Tonight we call for Volunteers. We need strong, brave, resourceful, adventurous rats. But most of all we need young rats.' His gaze explored the room, and I felt it brush me.

'Listen with care. The voyage will be long. It will be hard.'

'Stern defences guard the Unknown Land.' Pedro was speaking again, his deep voice urgent now. 'Around it sweeps the world's wildest, roughest ocean. Mighty icebergs patrol the water, slicing through an unwary ship like a blade through cheese. A barrier of ice circles the Land, coating the surface of the sea in frozen whiteness. Ice that can trap the strongest ship, crushing it to matchwood.

'Of the Land itself I shall not speak. But blizzards will blind your eyes and bite your tails and beat your fur into frozen sheets. You will feel colder than death. You may never return.

'And you will feel a greater excitement and joy than

you have ever dreamed of. You will see such wonders! Such beauty! Such sights! I cannot describe them.

'But I am going back. I am drawn south again, as if a rope was around my body winding me in, like an anchor to its hawsehole, like a fish on a line. Like a traveller going home.

'Come. Be one of the Volunteers! But only if you are certain.'

He stopped. Despite the warmth of that summer night we were shivering. Each of us gathered in the moonlight at the top of the Lighthouse, silent with our thoughts.

THREE

Of course we volunteered. Eddie and I didn't even discuss it. The Selection Committee asked us a few questions, checked that we were healthy, then said – nothing.

It was agony waiting, not knowing if we had been accepted. We talked about our chances, over and over. 'You'll be certain,' said Eddie, biting his long nails, in the way he did when he felt anxious. 'You're strong. You're a useful fighter. You're all action. Me – I'm too thin. I think too much.'

'You'll be fine,' I said. 'Maybe you're thin but you're wiry. And you're clever.'

The days went by and still we did not hear. The longing for adventure gripped me. I wanted to go on the Expedition more than anything in the world. I felt strangely drawn to the mysterious South. I dreamed of ice-covered seas, and the white-bound Land, its secrets all unknown. Eddie was the same. Sometimes we sat on the river bank in the sun surrounded by the hum of our great busy city, and talked about what we would do if one of us only was chosen. We couldn't bear the thought.

But that is what happened. I was chosen. Eddie wasn't. No discussion with the Committee, no chance to appeal. It was unbearable. 'You must go, Hackle, you know you must,' – Eddie pushed me gently towards the black ship. 'I'll get another chance another time. You can tell me all about it when you get back.' And he ran off.

So – at last – I climbed aboard, excited, proud, my family amazed. Yet my heart was heavy. I could not share the adventure with Eddie. But duties began at once and soon I was in the thick of it, hardly able to stop and think. There were meetings with the other Volunteers, jobs to do. Horses clattered up to the Dock pulling drayloads of stores. Hefties swarmed over the ship stowing gear. All was incredible bustle.

Finally I got a chance to slip on shore and look for Eddie. He was sitting with his sweetheart, Vanilla. 'I've found out who really decides who can come,' he whispered in my ear, so Vanilla couldn't hear. 'It's that fat hairy Old Clements. He once went on an expedition, and he likes young rats like you and me. I'm going to see him. I've got a plan.'

I went back to my duties hardly able to stand the waiting. Then suddenly I got a message. 'Cheer up, both going.' As simple as that. And the next thing I knew my best friend was on board. Oh, the release of happiness!

'We Volunteers need someone to tend to any illnesses,' grinned Eddie. 'Meet your newly appointed medical rat. Well, I do know some things about mending bodies. I learned them from my wise old great-aunt Lobelia.'

Proudly I showed Eddie over the ship. She was newly built, wooden, none of this modern iron, with three stubby masts and a coal-fired engine. Below in our special space the ship was a mass of heavy timber. Thick wooden frames and stiffeners, intersected by heavy beams and bulkheads. We'd never seen anything like it. Several of us Volunteers had done a bit of gnawing around a through-bolt to discover the thickness of the ship's sides. They were as thick as two of us measured nose to tail. Ice must be truly terrible to need such strength.

Then I took Eddie to the neat little nesting place I'd made in the jam and soup store and we drank from a pannikin of rum, to our success, and the future.

The day of departure came. Huge crowds jostled in the sunshine. Hefties made speeches. We Volunteers were all safely on board of course, checked off and numbered. We had celebrated our last parties with our friends. We had wandered the familiar streets and sniffed the old familiar smells for the very last time. We had said our goodbyes to our dear families. Blackwall and the Committee had wished each of us luck. My sisters had even been on board and seen our quarters.

Eddie had decided to get married at the very last moment to his sweetheart Vanilla. I had a girl, and now, just as we were leaving, I asked her to marry me – when I got back. She was a kind, sweet thing, called Clemmy, with big brown eyes, and she promised to wait for me. We managed to get Vanilla and Clemmy on board for the trip down river. They would have to get off before our ship left for the open sea but it was good to have a last few hours together and it would be a long, long time before we saw them again. If ever. But we tried not to think about that.

Our ship cast off from the wharf. The heavy Dock gates swung open. I'm a true ships' rat. My soul lifts when the gangplank goes up. A thin strip of water begins to glint between the ship and land, widens – and we are separated. The crowds cheered, whistles tooted, hooters and sirens blew. What a wonderful racket! What a start to the voyage! Our hearts swelled with pride. The Expedition had begun. 'Sort out the world for us while we're gone,' shouted Fergal, a broad-shouldered contented-looking young rat standing next to me. We laughed.

'Where's she bound for?' I heard a ships' rat cry, as we passed through the Dock gates. 'Why, to the South Pole, of course,' replied his friend.

We moved with the tide down river. Each ship we passed hooted, and whistled, and dipped ensigns, and everyone cheered us. It was good to be part of such a great Expedition. Good to be alive!

FOUR

We didn't really settle down until we had waved goodbye to old England. Then it was the dip and roll of the open ocean, the smell of salt spray, the joyful regular rhythm of days at sea.

Blackwall and the Seniors had appointed a Voyage Leader. He was handsome, athletic, very proud of his muscular body. We called him The Commander. Now Sly-eye Shaver, the top Scout, marched through the ship announcing the First Briefing.

All of us Volunteers scuttled fast along the rat-runs. It wouldn't do to be late. Our meeting place was well chosen, between the solid oak stiffeners well forward in the bow, behind casks of salted beef and split peas. A private space far too tight for snooping Hefties.

The Commander was already in place, watching us arrive. The Scouts stood behind. Sly-eye Shaver called the roll. We Volunteers eyed each other, still learning who everyone was.

The Commander gave out the Sea Orders. We were to be divided into watches, with set duties. There was to be no slacking. We were to stay fit, prepare ourselves for what lay ahead. Races up the rigging, distance training, night climbing, competitive fighting, Ginger Days (we groaned inwardly – everything done at the double). Once a week there would be a Patching Day when we saw to our things, made sure everything was shipshape. A sort of day off: an old Naval tradition.

The Commander was strict. He wanted to keep us at it.

After the Briefing Eddie and I nosed around in the Sail Locker. I needed a good chew on a length of rope – we have to keep our teeth sharp.

'I don't think The Commander knows about frozen countries,' said Eddie suddenly. 'I think he's like us. Keen, eager, but ignorant.'

Eddie put into words what was bothering me. We didn't question our Orders, of course. That wasn't the ships' rats' way. The Commander was obviously brainy, but none of us knew how he would do things, or come to his decisions.

'And what about Pedro?' said Eddie. 'He was standing with the rest of us. He isn't even a Scout. But he's the only one who's been to the Unknown Land.'

'Let's try and talk to him,' I said. 'We need to find out things before we get there.'

'We can ask The Pilot as well,' said Eddie. 'He's been to the cold countries in the north. He knows about the cold. And Kettles. That extra-long tea-drinking friend of his. He's an old Polar hand.'

We laughed. Kettles and The Pilot were always together, one long and thin, the other short and stout.

I looked around for a good length of chewing rope to take back to our nest. Our discussion had made me feel better. If I've got a worry I like to do something about it straight away.

Suddenly we heard the heavy tread of approaching Hefties. I dropped my rope and ran.

Our ship turned out to have a roll like a decoy duck. And she leaked. Stinking water started sloshing around our quarters in the holds. Not what we'd hoped for. The Hefties discovered the leak and it was mess and danger for days while they shifted stores and threw away spoiled food. Every time we join a ship we have to learn what our batch of Hefties are like. This lot worked hard. There weren't many of them, but they were always somewhere, and we had to be constantly on our guard.

Blackwall was right. It was a long, long voyage. But at last we had sailed far enough south for serious gales. Now the ship lurched and kicked in mountainous waves. Sea after sea broke over the decks. Plates smashed, drawers shot open, clothes flung around. The Hefties and their things were permanently sodden. We mostly stayed below out of danger but we enjoyed checking the mess.

Late one night after coming off watch I joined a gang of mates under the fo'c'sle to swap stories of voyages past. The light from a lamp jumped and flickered. An oilskin hanging on a hook swayed rhythmically with the rolling of the ship. Billy Stumps, a tough rat from down river, gripped a sleeve and, swinging in time to our thumping feet, began a stirring rendition of the Sailor's Lament. Adapted to our needs of course. He'd just got to

> The sailor died
> Our Hackle cried

when the ship lurched violently. The sleeve of the oilskin touched the lamp, the flame licked across and flared up. Billy leaped off, his fur nastily singed. The yellow flames spread rapidly along the woodwork.

Fire! Fire on a wooden ship is our greatest dread. We raced into Emergency Drill. Scouts spread the alarm, monitored the Risk Level, stood at key points. The rest of us took up our Disaster Stations. Jaws set, bodies tense, waiting orders. Hefties hurried on deck in confusion, shouting, running.

Nothing we could do would save the ship. Everything had to depend on the Hefties. A horrible chilling way to face death – blood racing for action, but no action possible. The ship lumbered along in the immense waves, squalls shrieking in the rigging. The night was pitch black. Our chances if we had to abandon ship were zero. That wasn't official. But I knew.

Then I smelled the blessed sour smell of wet burnt wood. The Hefties had got the fire out. Our Scouts sounded Alarm Over.

I climbed up the mast. I wanted to clear my head. The ship slid down the side of each great swell, and lurched soddenly up the next. The squalling wind lashed my wet fur.

Down in the water I saw something floating, large and pale. The body of a dead Hefty. Not one of ours. It had been drowned a long time. But out here in the great empty ocean the dead Hefty looked so very lonely. It made me feel very sad.

FIVE

Finally we reached port. It wasn't particularly big, but it was worth waiting for, after so much time at sea. The ship's leak had to be fixed so everything was unloaded out of the holds and work started on repairs. That meant a good long Shore Leave, the dream of all ships' rats. Days and nights in a foreign port! Meet the locals, parties, dancing, new food, that kind of thing. 'About time,' winked Fergal, as we swaggered into town.

The local ships' rats were truly friendly. We were heroes, even though we hadn't yet been south to the Unknown Land. It was enough that we were going. Eddie and I wished that our sweethearts were with us to share the good times. Fergal fell in love. Much good that was, with us leaving so soon.

We returned from Shore Leave to find the ship bunged up with more stores, crammed like a dustman's cart. A flock of terrified sheep ran and bleated astern. Worst of all there were dogs. Big hairy vicious dogs. We hadn't seen anything like them. They howled with excitement. Pedro explained that they were sledge dogs, trained to work in the snow. Each was chained amidships just out of reach of its neighbour. We could skitter around them though, and the sight of us moving just past their noses drove them mad. Their lips drew back, showing terrible teeth.

The very next night as Eddie and I were walking along the wharf something – a kind of instinct – made me jump sideways behind a crate. Eddie ducked after. Cautiously I peered out. Just ahead two rats were leaning against a bollard. Not our kind. But brown!

I hadn't given a thought to our enemies. Now here they were, big heavy-bodied brutes, their horrible small ears almost hidden in their harsh shaggy fur.

Where had they come from? Were these the only two? Did they know our plans? The questions tumbled round my head. There was no time to lose. I was nifty, and I loved a fight. Eddie was extremely useful for his weight. But brown rats are much stronger and heavier than us. If only we had reinforcements.

'Let's watch them,' Eddie was whispering in my ear. 'We might learn something.' He was right. Our enemies had obviously been drinking. Grog would slow their reactions. Then we noticed their ship. It had just come alongside ours, a dirty tub of a vessel. That gave us real hope. Perhaps they didn't know where we were heading for. Yet.

I chose the one with a kink in his tail. Eddie chose Scar-ear. 'Fighting together. Ships' rats forever,' I hissed. Then we jumped them.

The two rats swung around heavily, snarling, teeth bared. But their aim was clumsy. We ducked, swerved, and were in, biting, rolling, kicking. We got them down, and finished them off. Grabbing them by their legs we tossed their bodies into the water.

Quickly we reported to The Commander. He called a Council of War.

'We must guard our ship against any intruding brown rat, and ourselves against attack.' The Commander spoke precisely, and fast. 'We are a chosen band. We cannot afford to lose anyone. On the good side we leave tomorrow. And these brown rats are likely to be low-grade louts. Their vessel is a dirty tub.

'On the bad side we cannot prevent our enemies finding out about our plans. The port is full of gossip. Some fool will talk. From this moment we go on full alert. Strict watch will be mounted. No one will leave the ship without an exceptional reason.

'Guard yourselves! Guard each other.'

The Commander was turning out to be a rat of action. That is what was needed.

We got away from the wharf next day with no more crises. But our nerves were stretched taut. The humans

22

celebrated with bands and cheering crowds. We were too busy and anxious to join in. As we moved down the harbour our Scouts checked all corners of the ship for stowaways. The report came. 'Ship clear.' We began relaxing.

But high above our heads something terrible was happening. Lashed to the mainmast was a wooden barrel, a Hefty look-out place reached by a ladder, and a trapdoor. One of our Scouts had crept with great bravery amongst the celebrating Hefties, and climbed up the mast to the wooden barrel. And there he found what we had all feared. A brown rat spy. They fought, bodies locked. Blinded with battle, they missed their footing and tumbled down, down. They hit the deck with a sickening thud; and died instantly.

The Hefties threw the bodies overboard. We mourned the loss of our brave companion. Sadness filled our hearts. None of us could think about the voyage ahead. We could only think of our loved ones on the other side of the world.

We were not free yet from the brown rat danger. Unexpectedly we put into port again and sacks of dirty coal were loaded onto the already overcrowded deck.

Gloomily we mounted watch round the clock, guarding against enemies attempting to get aboard. Gloomily we listened to The Pilot. He'd checked the ship and estimated the overloading at Highest Risk. We were about to enter the world's roughest, wildest ocean. What chance did we have in a bad blow! And gloomily we sloshed around in the hold. We thought the leak had been fixed. But it hadn't.

One thing happened to cheer us up. A strong cheerful ships' rat climbed aboard amongst the coal bags, and volunteered to take our dead companion's place. He said his name was Jonas. He was taken to The Commander who interviewed him; and we welcomed him into our band of Volunteers.

Then, at last, we were truly on our way. We had checked the ship from stern to bow, from mast top to deepest holds, and we were certain that no spying brutish enemies lurked aboard. Nothing could stop us leaving now. Our real work was beginning. We put all thoughts of our dear loved ones from us.

The land with all its colours, its sweet grass, its swaying trees and soul-catching smells, faded behind us. Our last links were broken. We would do something worth the doing before we saw it again.

We faced the unknown South.

SIX

Miracle of miracles, we passed through that wild tempestuous southern ocean with no storms. The long swells followed one behind the other, great hills and valleys of water. Our desperately overloaded ship laboured, rolling so heavily the tip of the mainmast sometimes dipped beneath a foam-flecked wave. A few wretched sheep were washed overboard. Enormous albatrosses ceaselessly skimmed the sea's surface, searching for food. We knew how to keep out of the Hefties' sight – that was our way of life. But we were the right size for an albatross dinner.

The Hefties shivered as they stood watch. The remaining sheep huddled forlornly. One night snow whirled through the air, and the light from the lamps picked out the flakes spiralling in the blackness. The dogs chained on deck howled long, lonely howls.

And still we sailed on south, south, where ships did not venture, as if drawn by an invisible rope towards the waiting – something; I don't know what it was. But I felt strangely alert, filled with anticipation.

Not all Volunteers felt this way. Some preferred to stay warmly down below on their time off, drinking, singing, sleeping. But some were like me, tense, waiting. Every moment spare from duties I climbed up to a stack of timber lashed to the fore skid beams high above the deck. A good meeting place for like-minded mates. We huddled against the frigid wind and biting cold, whiskers blown backwards, ears blown inside out, discussing all that we had discovered so far about the Unknown Land.

Eddie had been looking after a rat called Skelly who'd hurt his arm in the Engine Room. A dangerous noisy place to be, but Skelly liked seeing how things worked. Skelly came up to our meeting place with his friend Padders. Padders was always winning The Commander's rigging races. Now he hooked his long strong tail around a wire and swung out above the heads of the cold Hefties lurching along the heaving deck below.

> The Hefties work
> While we rats shirk
> Hoorah for ships' rats
> Ha!

shouted Padders, into the whistling wind. A good new mate, this Padders!

We had bets who would see the first iceberg. Skelly won. I was below scoffing bacon rinds when he came tumbling down the ladder in his eagerness to tell, almost damaging his arm again. We raced up on deck, forgetting to beware Hefties.

The iceberg was huge, real. By evening we were surrounded by icebergs. Their deeply cracked sides glowed a mysterious blue. Water boomed in the hollows of their caves. I gazed, spellbound. The icebergs belonged. We were the outsiders.

In the night I woke. There was a strange scraping, sighing, rustling sound, as if something was alive just beyond the planking of the hull. I hurried on deck. Small lumps of ice were streaming past, ghostly white in the black water.

We were entering the ice. We had truly arrived. I woke Eddie and we climbed up to our timber stack and watched, eyes aching, bodies shivering, but we couldn't stop.

By the morning our world had changed. For ever. The ship was moving forward, but it seemed to be riding over a glittering white icy plain. The swell, the sounds of wind and wave, all had gone. The deep ocean lay just beneath, but forgotten. Sometimes the ice was whipped into peaks, like pure white meringue. Sometimes it was smooth as sand after the tide has gone out. Sometimes it heaped up into chaotic piles.

The Hefties rushed around excitedly, pointing, shouting. Eddie and I were desperate to know more. We searched for Pedro, and found him stretched out along the bowsprit. We hung on next to him, staring down at the ice. Our ship was driving forward jerkily, twisting, searching for gaps. Sometimes we barged a floe, the ship's strong bow climbing on the ice and leaning until it cracked, a black line shooting ahead, splitting the white.

Crash! Thud! Shove! What a ride! Great blocks of broken ice tipped and fell sideways, and reared up again, scraping and grating against our sides.

'Ice is hard. Harder than the hardest rock,' said Pedro. 'Don't ever forget. It all looks harmless. But this is pack ice and it's dangerous. It can break up with no warning. Pieces of ice can start grinding together with terrible force. I know. I've seen it.' There was silence. 'I think The Commander does not want to ask,' he said quietly. 'I think he wants to find it all out for himself.'

The ship stopped with a sickening shock, quivering in every timber, masts and rigging rattling. We peered down.

We'd hit a thick piece of ice which tilted slowly, revealing a green flank continuing deep into the clear water. Far below we could see a long cruel spike of ice reaching out. We shuddered.

That night we had a Feast, celebrating our entry into the pack ice. The Pilot and Kettles organised everything with great style. The sheep had been slaughtered and their carcasses hung from the rigging where they froze – nature's refrigerator, as Jonas said. So there was meat for the taking. We drank a toast to our success, with both feet up on the table – an old Naval custom, announced The Pilot, when first entering the true Polar regions.

I longed to be the first to see land. Staring out across the pack ice I saw clouds that looked like land, and land that turned into icebergs. But late one evening as I gazed south from the top spar on the foremast I saw the blue outline of high mountain peaks on the horizon. The Unknown Land!

The thrill of it! I was just an ordinary young riverside rat. I'd travelled, yes. But nothing like this. Eddie climbed up and we sat looking and looking. The sun filled the hours that should have been dark with unexpected, beautiful colours – skies stained lemon-yellow with pale green edges, clouds dyed red and purple. Calm patches of water between the floes shimmered with all the colours in the sky, and the ice glowed a soft lavender-blue. The sun shone on the snowy peaks of the distant mountains and they seemed to glitter like purest gold.

The land came slowly closer. What would happen to us there? Who could tell?

SEVEN

'Hackle! Wake up!' Eddie was prodding me hard. '*Wake up!* We're going on shore. Now! With Pedro. We've got permission.'

We had reached land. It wasn't the distant golden mountains, but a bleak rocky cape. Others had been chosen to be the first ashore with the Hefties. But not me. They went, hidden in the whaleboat. I had gazed at all I could see, but I couldn't see much: only an icy barren shore, and a stony, lonely beach backed by a high steep cliff. I couldn't bear missing out so I crept away to sleep.

Now I raced after Eddie. The whaleboat had returned and was tied alongside. A quick check for Hefties, all clear, and we slid down a rope, jumped on board, and hid behind some bags stuffed under a seat. Rule-breaking behaviour, but there was no time to find anywhere safer. Hefties climbed in, their heavy bodies rocking the boat, then we were off, pushing through pieces of bumping ice. The keel scraped on gravel. The Hefties reached under the seat for their bags, grabbing and feeling in their eagerness to be gone.

'Wait for Pedro,' whispered Eddie. 'He'll guide us.'

Pedro eased himself out from a safe hiding place under the planking. He stood gazing at the beach, as if his soul was feeding. He took in deep gulps of air. 'Ah!' he said. 'Penguins! That smell again!'

The beach was crammed with thousands and thousands of squawking penguins. Squwaarkk! Squawk, squawk! The din was incredible. So was the smell.

'They'll go for you but we can move faster.' Pedro was giving instructions. 'Watch *above* your heads. There are birds here – big dangerous brutes with beaks like daggers. They've plenty of penguin eggs and chicks to gorge on so they should leave us alone. Good luck. Follow me.' And he was off, jumping over lumps of ice and on to the shore.

I wanted to stop, and kiss the ground. My first steps on the Unknown Land!

But Pedro was running between heaps of pebbles where penguins sat on their eggs, past chicks like grey fluffy bags, squeaking in terror, past the jabbing beaks and lashing bony flippers of their angry, squawking parents. The ground was browny-red with their excreta and the stink was overwhelming. Eddie and I streaked after, keeping low to the ground, never taking our eyes off Pedro. Suddenly he skidded around some wooden crates and disappeared through a small hole. We followed and found ourselves – inside a hut.

We couldn't believe it. We had come to an unknown Land. What in the name of all Great Rats was this?

Pedro was lying on a crate watching our faces and laughing. 'Welcome to my old home,' he said. 'I and my two companions slept here in this storeroom. We had plenty of food' – he waved his hand towards boxes piled against the wooden walls. 'Now come and see the Hefties' living hut.'

We followed him along a narrow short tunnel up into a crowded space filled with the stuff of Hefty lives. The astonishing thing was the look of the place. Everything was as if it had just been put down. Nothing rotten or decayed. Half-opened tins of food and half-eaten biscuits lay on the table. Clothes hung on hooks. It seemed as if the owners had only stepped outside a moment before.

Eddie burrowed into one of the bunks. 'We could live here for years! What's wrong with it?'

I nosed over the table looking for a memento to take back to the ship, some little thing to remind me of what I had seen. Perhaps something useful for our future work. I couldn't decide, so I ate a biscuit instead. It was hard, frozen, good for my teeth. And it still tasted of biscuit.

But Pedro was hurrying us on. Outside the hut lay a wonderland of rubbish, a heaven of discarded things. All scattered around as if thrown away yesterday. Pedro wouldn't let us enjoy it. He was running towards the steep cliff at the back of the beach, weaving between the penguins and their heaps of pebbles and squeaking chicks. We followed, deafened by the squawking, ducking the pecks of angry birds, and started climbing. Up, up, slipping as we climbed, past penguins balancing on scraps of flatness and little ledges.

Suddenly Pedro pushed us under a rock. 'Beware!' He pointed up at strong-bodied birds with piercing eyes hovering along the cliffside, screeching angrily. 'Skuas. Their nests are somewhere near. They'll go for us if they see us.' And he led us on a slower route using rocks as cover. We stopped once for a quick feed, a penguin egg each, extremely good eating. 'Ah!' said Pedro, licking his whiskers. 'I've been dreaming about that.'

The climb was hard but we reached the top. Behind us was the sea. In front stretched my first proper view of the new Land. At last.

It was after midnight and the sun shone low in the sky with the same golden beauty as last night. But it shone on a terrible scene. Huge boulders lay scattered about as if tossed carelessly down by giants. Mountains gripped in perpetual ice rose beyond, and beyond again, into the furthest distance. It was a white wasteland. A desolate, silent, empty, frozen desert.

We understood now why Pedro's Hefties hadn't stayed living on the lonely stony beach. The place was a prison. On all sides except one the sea beat against the shore. The only way out was the cliff, with at the top this frozen desert, and the impassible ice-covered mountains beyond.

Pedro walked slowly to a great boulder and stood beneath its rough curve with bowed head. Eddie and I crouched against the cold; silent, puzzled.

Pedro turned to us. Tears welled in his eyes. 'Here lies my noble friend Nico. He died here, in this Unknown Land. He was brave and honourable. We went through much together.'

He turned back to the boulder. 'I and my remaining companion buried Nico here. The ground was ice-hard. It took many hours of labour.'

The biting wind sliced into my skin as if I had no fur. My naked ears throbbed. Eddie bit his nails, and rubbed his freezing tail.

'Thank you for being with me,' said Pedro. 'I had to come back.'

We scrambled down the cliff, crossed the beach, and we reached the whaleboat just in time. The Hefties were scrunching towards us across the ice and rocks.

It was now long past midnight. But our first adventure

in the new Land had been so full of unexpected things I could not sleep. I thought about Pedro's brave friend Nico lying buried on the cliff top in this dreadful lonely place. Pedro said that his remaining companion had died of a mysterious illness on the voyage home. So he was the only survivor.

I crept to the bow. Our ship was under way. Behind us, clouds rolled in over the cape and met, like locking fists. The land was hidden, as if it never existed.

A fast tide swept enormous blocks of ice racing past, as if they weighed nothing. I watched them crash against a line of icebergs ahead, grinding on top of each other, breaking in heaps. The blocks of ice surrounded our ship, jostling us, crowding us in. With horror I realised that we, too, were being forced towards the waiting icebergs.

We could not stop. We were doomed. I turned to raise the alarm. But The Commander was standing behind me, watching grim-faced.

'There is no point,' he said. 'We cannot abandon ship. Survival in this water is impossible. We would freeze. We must go down with our ship. There is no other way.'

I understood that cruel fact, with bitter certainty.

We watched mesmerised. I could hear the crash and grind of ice being forced on ice, see the high bulk and icicle-fringed face of the nearest berg. Above us the Hefties struggled to keep the ship free of the crushing ice floes, the unyielding icebergs. And slowly, almost without our realising it, the tide eased. The ice floes trapping us began to unlock. We began to get free.

'We have entered a new kind of battleground,' said

The Commander. 'This enemy is all-powerful. We are helpless and weak. It has been a hard lesson for me,' he muttered, biting his lower lip.

EIGHT

Suddenly the world changed to brilliant blue skies and glittering beauty. The sun glared. The air smelled as fresh as the first day that ever was. Our ship sailed amongst sparkling white floes on an indigo-blue sea. Seals lay on the ice, scratching their bellies. Penguins ran up and stared. Birds swooped and whales curved their great backs out of the water, blowing spouts of fishy spray. Everywhere there was life!

The light was so clear it was as if blinkers had been pulled from our eyes, and we were looking over the curve of the Earth. The sun shone on mighty mountain ranges and vast wrinkled glaciers. We even thought that we saw smoke rising from a mountain far to the south. Pedro said we were right. Here, amongst all this ice, was a volcano.

Pedro smiled at our confusion. The Unknown Land does this, he said. It can switch in seconds. From forbidding freezing fog to intense sun, from harsh rejection to indifference, from safety to danger.

The Commander granted us all two Patching Days – two full days off. We found places to stretch out in the sun's warmth. But happiness was dangerous. We relaxed our guard. Several Volunteers had nasty near misses with Hefties.

Eddie and I had been examining our coats. They were definitely growing longer and thicker. Our bodies were adjusting better to the cold. Our ears, paws, feet, tails – all the areas of bare skin were toughening up. We decided to move our sleeping place outside, as an experiment. Exploring cautiously, we found a large square wicker basket amongst the deck cargo, with a canvas pocket attached on the inside. We shredded up a book we found in the pocket, to make a comfortable nest.

We felt very hopeful. We'd come to discover whether ships' rats could settle in this new land. When our ship worked into a small ice-filled inlet between rounded hills we rushed to get permission to go ashore. Perhaps here we would find a new home.

The Commander granted leave to everyone. 'Discover what you can,' he said. 'Every rat for himself.'

The Hefties jumped from ice floe to ice floe then on to the land. We hadn't even tried being on the ice. 'We'll show up horribly against that whiteness,' said Eddie anxiously. 'And where can we hide? Where are our escape routes? We shouldn't move without an escape route planned.'

But we had to risk it, or not go. We waited until the last Hefty disappeared then lowered ourselves gingerly on to the nearest floe. To our surprise it was covered in soft fluffy snow. But it had hummocky bits and hollows which helped us feel safer as we ran across to the edge.

'It's just a question of floe-hopping,' I said, trying to sound confident. Our floe rocked up and down. The floe next to it rocked, but not in time. I leaped over the gap and scrabbled on board. Action for me was generally better than worrying.

We got better at dashing, judging gaps, leaping. The last bit was the worst. A ledge of slippery ice stuck out from the shore, washed by waves. We were soaked. But we had reached land!

We scuttled for the nearest rocks. As long as there were dark places to hide our dark bodies, we felt secure. Bare earth showed amongst the rocks. Except it wasn't proper earth but a kind of fine loose stuff. The rocks were strangely split, each fragment balancing next to the piece it once belonged to. Like the bones of a skeleton, or a loaf of bread in slices. But each rested clear and undisturbed on the ground. Not buried by leaves, or twined by tendrils, or pushed aside by roots. And then I realised. *Nothing* was growing here.

It made me feel very strange. This was our world, but not our world. The sun warmed the rocks and that felt familiar. But no insects buzzed in the air. No beetle skittered away. There were no smells that I knew. This world was pure, and silent.

We explored along the hills until we could look down on the head of the inlet. It was a cosy, sheltered place. After all the immensity we'd been sailing through the inlet seemed idyllic. 'We *could* live here, Eddie!' I said happily. There were no buildings, of course. No roads, no jetty, nothing like that. But we could imagine them here, and us living comfortable lives. In this protected safe little place the awful hugeness of the Unknown Land was suddenly shut out.

But we had to go. We never knew when the ship would depart. We had to be constantly vigilant.

On the way back Eddie discovered running water. A tiny stream flowing over stones, just like happened in the rest of the world. We drank and drank. Then, by the side of a boulder, I made a second wonderful discovery. Moss! Something green and growing was here in this Land after all. We rolled in its softness. We pushed our noses in and sank our paws deep inside. Then we lay on the mound of moss smelling the true smell of life.

So now our idyllic place had everything. I bit off a piece of moss to take back to the ship as a treasure.

When we reached the shore, the ice floes for some reason were swaying up and down like pontoons, and beginning to move apart. Eddie and I stared in horror. But we had to reach the ship. We began leaping and running across the ice as best we could.

Half-way back we faced a gap too wide to jump. Every

second the floe we were on moved further away from its neighbour.

'We've got to swim, we can stand the coldness if we're fast,' instructed Eddie. I leaped in. The cold hit like a hammer. My head throbbed. I struck out for the next floe and scrambled up, my body shivering uncontrollably. Eddie had already landed – 'Move to get your circulation going,' he shouted – and raced off. The danger of being seen no longer mattered. We had to reach the ship.

But the floe we had landed on with such effort was a trap. It began sweeping along, swaying and rocking, away from the ship, heading towards open water. Eddie and I huddled together, terrified. It was like being on a cart pulled by a bolting horse. We could not get off.

Suddenly our floe swung round, and rammed into a big floe. In that instant we leaped with all our strength and landed on the new floe. No sooner done than our old floe swung around again and was off on its travels.

We lay gathering our breath. We had been lucky indeed. The new big floe was out of the current, and gave us a route back to the ship. From unexpected danger to sudden safety. No warning. Just as Pedro said.

We climbed on board with shaking legs, and a real need. Food! We found it – a good feed of sardines, and bread and butter, leftovers from a Hefty supper, lying on the wardroom table.

The Commander ordered a Roll Call. All Volunteers were safely back, though several had dangerous returns to the ship, like Eddie and me.

Before I went to sleep I put my precious piece of moss safely on a ledge. I needed to know it was there, if things got tough.

NINE

Our Scouts stood by ready to jump into a whaleboat at a moment's notice, determined to get ashore at every opportunity.

But I didn't envy them their next chance. Biter and Sly-eye Shaver squeezed into an overcrowded boat as the Hefties rowed off amongst monstrous grounded icebergs. The icebergs had tilted sides and tops crumbling like old cheese.

Ahead surf sucked and thrashed on to a dark shelving beach. Penguins swarmed, crying their wild cries which grew louder and louder, then faded away to silence, and began over again, in waves of lonely sound. The Hefties beached the whaleboat through the surf and milled around.

Biter and Shaver didn't dare get out of the boat. The place was infested with great screeching skuas so they hid and observed what they could. The Hefties set up a wooden post amongst the squabbling penguins and their reeking nests. But when they tried to launch the whaleboat the heavy swell threw it around like a plank of wood. The soaked, shivering Hefties pulled grimly at the oars.

Our Scouts were mightily relieved to get back to the ship. Penguins and skuas might be able to survive in a place like that, they reported, but it was useless for us.

Still the Hefties kept our ship driving on. We sailed past awesome cliffs of ice which stretched into the distance like an endless glittering wall. The swell roared and pounded against the ice cliffs, throwing spray high. This Unknown Country was huge all right. Immense.

The days were getting colder. No doubt about it. The water the Hefties used to clean the decks each morning froze and they had to shovel it up as ice. They grumbled and swore. One morning ice even formed over the sea, a coating like grey grease which thickened too fast for our liking. Where were we heading? We felt very uneasy.

Then to our relief the ship turned and we went back the way we had come. Except suddenly, we stopped. Of all places, in a gap in the great ice cliffs.

A few Hefties immediately set off across the snowy surface pulling a sledge. Pedro went with them, hidden amongst their gear. We felt jealous, but as the only one of us with local experience he had the right to go.

The Commander was itching for action. He chose

three Scouts and went exploring. They didn't get far. The light was peculiar, all glary. Like being inside a glass of milk, said Biter. They kept falling over bumps in the snow they couldn't see, and came back on board very annoyed.

No one else had permission to go ashore until Pedro returned and reported back. We consoled ourselves exploring the cabin of a sledging Hefty. Suddenly we were jolted off our feet by a tremendous grating, scraping noise, then a truly sickening shock. Every beam and frame in the ship groaned. A fat rat called Tankey was knocked clean off the Hefty's bunk by the force of the blow.

We rushed on deck and saw a smallish iceberg rolling by, right next to us, seething and hissing. Its hard seamed surface looked like the hide of some monstrous animal. Hefties ran around with scared faces. We began Emergency Drill, crouching tensely in our Disaster Stations.

Everything was strangely quiet. There were no more fearful noises. Our Scouts were carrying out checks, we knew that.

The Alarm Over sounded. The iceberg had only grazed us. But the force had been enough to wrench a large piece of solid oak out of our hull. We could see it bobbing in the water.

Eddie and I were truly tired. It was getting too cold to sleep out on deck, but we decided to spend one last night in our basket. We snuggled down trying not to think about sharp spikes of green ice, hard as rock, for ever lurking in the water.

The next thing we knew we were swaying and lurching through the air, then dropping heavily with a jarring thud. We peered through the wickerwork. It was morning and we were out on the snow. Hefties were fussing around a strange large object lying flat on a tarpaulin, which they attached to our basket. Slowly the object began to swell, then rise. Our basket moved in an unnatural jerky way.

Suddenly the Hefty Leader jumped in, cramming next to us. The basket rose up off the snow straight into the air! The Hefty Leader leaned down and picked up bags of sand lying in the bottom of the basket. He threw them over the edge. We shot upwards so fast my stomach was left behind. The basket jerked then began to go round and round.

Eddie was very sick. His eyes were tight shut.

I was watching though. 'Hold on Eddie, we're coming down.' I squeezed his arm. 'There's a wire rope, and Hefties are pulling us.' We bumped on the ground. Rough Hefty hands held the basket. The Hefty Leader got out. Everything felt as if it was still swaying. Then a different Hefty climbed in and up we went again.

I edged under the flap of our pocket and looked out. For a blissful moment, I knew what it was to be a bird. We were hovering high in the sky. Our ship lay far below, ridiculously small, moored in a dark crack of water between the ice cliffs. Tiny figures of Hefties moved across the snow.

Eagerly I turned towards the south. Eddie's eyes were still tight shut. 'Look, Eddie, look!' I urged. 'It's the

Unknown Land. We can truly see it.'

We looked with our bird's eyes, and saw an unending white plain – simply unending. Solid. Smooth. But all white. All snow and ice. With no end. Nothing. We could see no change, not even at the horizon.

The Hefties pulled the basket down and our Hefty got out. Eddie and I sat dazed. We had been flying. If nothing else ever happened, this was enough.

We crept out while the Hefties ate their lunch. The Pilot, who had spent time in a Naval Store Yard, explained that we had been in a balloon. The Commander was desperate to have a turn. He climbed into the basket, fidgeting impatiently. But the wind began blowing. The huge balloon swayed and tugged on its rope. The Hefties let it flatten again, until it was limp, and useless. They left everything lying behind on the ice and went off to kill seals.

The Commander jumped out angrily. 'It's just as well,' said The Pilot. 'He shouldn't risk his life up in that thing. Much too dangerous. It could drop out of the sky like a stone and then where would we be?'

The Hefties who had gone on the sledge journey came back. We hung around, longing to talk to Pedro about his adventure. But Pedro didn't want to talk. He was tired. All he would say was, 'I got the furthest south.'

'Furthest south?' Why would anyone want to do that? Eddie and I puzzled about what he could mean.

TEN

'I reckon the Hefties are up to something,' said The Pilot a few days later. We were eating a late supper behind the stove in the galley. 'I reckon they're looking for a place to stop, properly. They've got plans.' The Pilot gnawed on a piece of fried seal. 'There's lots of stuff on this ship they haven't used. There's enough here to last them years. So our time is coming.'

'The Commander's got plans too,' said Kettles. The Pilot chuckled. 'But he should wait and see. At the ends of the Earth the winds and weather rule. Not Hefties. Not rats. That's what we old Polar rats say.'

The best laid plans
of rats and men
depend on the wind and the weather.
If the weather's bad
and the wind blows cruel
we'll all go down together!

Kettles and The Pilot sang this song through three times, then rolled off to bed.

Our ship was sailing past strange tumbling tongues of glacier, and dark gritty rocks. The volcano we'd seen weeks before rose beside us, its massive sloping sides seamed with ice, steam puffing from its crater in a lazy plume. I wondered if we might feel warmer next to the volcano, but we didn't.

The Pilot was right, though. The very next day we moored against the ice in a small sheltered bay. But in a most unsatisfactory way. The ship kept coming unstuck from our anchorage, drifting, then bumping back, timbers groaning and squeaking.

The Hefties began unloading some of their things. They swarmed through the ship shifting and lifting, disturbing our private spaces. It was exciting. Unsettling. We wanted to know what was happening. We wanted The Commander to tell us the plans. But The Commander kept silent, shut up in his private space.

At last a Briefing was announced. As we ran to the Meeting Place I noticed that ice was forming on the water which sloshed around our rat runs, from the ever-present ship's leak.

The Commander's voice was tight. 'The situation is as yet unclear. Scouts are out ascertaining the facts. No one is to leave the ship without permission. That is all.'

We huddled in corners exchanging rumours. Some of us were sure we were going to disembark tomorrow. Do not believe it, said others. The ship departs with everyone tomorrow. Billy Stumps announced that the Hefties had found the local humans. They lived in caves of ice and were covered in hair to keep themselves warm. Then there was the constant worry about the animals living here in the Unknown Country. Huge white bears prowled the frozen North, The Pilot had seen them. Well, Jonas reckoned, they were definitely here as well. He'd seen footprints in the snow of an ice floe, made by a huge animal, like a bear.

Eddie and I shinned up the rigging to spy out the land. We could see some Hefties digging painfully slow holes in the ground with pickaxes. We watched them banging in wooden posts – the very timber we'd sat amongst in our look-out place on the fore skid beams.

'They're building a hut!' I whistled. 'We don't need to be Scouts to work that out.'

The Hefties had chosen a flat place covered in small rubbly stones for their hut. Beyond were bare dark hills, and away in the distance high snow-gripped mountains. The views were huge. Difficult for me to manage. This place was so cold, so magnificent. It wasn't like the snug little inlet Eddie and I had chosen for ourselves, where we'd found the moss, and the running water.

Now The Commander called another Briefing. This time the plans came.

'Our Scouts have reported. The Hefties are building one large hut to live in, with two smaller huts.' (I nudged Eddie.) 'As soon as the Hefties have disembarked for the huts the ship will depart.

'A picked band of Volunteers will go ashore to the huts and continue the important work we came here to do. Can we live in this Unknown Land? We must find out. The work will be hard, conditions dangerous and tough. Sharing quarters in the huts with the Hefties will be difficult. The shore-based party will therefore be small. All other Volunteers will stay on board, and leave with the ship. Messages must be got back to our Leader Blackwall and the Committee. Reinforcements will need to be sent to those of us living here.

'The list of Stayers is being prepared now. Those of us moving on to the land must be ready to disembark at a moment's notice.'

The Commander didn't discuss things. This was it.

At least we knew what was going to happen. But none of us had ever dreamed that our band of Volunteers would be broken up.

Eddie and I wanted desperately to stay, despite Vanilla and Clemmy waiting for us back home. It wasn't easy to explain and we didn't try. But we each of us knew. Our lives were here. Not back there. The rest of the world felt far distant. Volunteers were being chosen for the great adventure.

We didn't want to be sent back. Our place was

here. That is why we had come.

The Unknown Land was winding its way into our souls. Just like Pedro had said, at that faraway meeting in the Lighthouse, by the banks of our dear great river.

ELEVEN

The Commander still hadn't announced the names of the Stayers. So we were all tense and fidgety. The Hefties seemed to be just as tense. Their huts were taking a long time to finish. At least they shifted the dogs off the ship and chained them to kennels built in a straggly line on the hillside. Good riddance. At last the decks were free and we could move around in some safety.

Then, with no warning, The Commander announced a new plan. A small party was to go exploring, he said. We Volunteers needed to see how fast we could travel, what was beyond the land we were moored against, that kind of thing. As we were going to live in this land we had better get on with it.

Eddie and I didn't know anything about exploring. But we were keen. That's all that mattered. Of course we volunteered. We were ships' rats and there's nothing a ships' rat can't do. In any case we thought it was a test and we wanted desperately to be chosen to stay. Scouts Biter and Lasher volunteered as well. The Commander said that two teams were enough to choose between and flipped a pebble.

We won. We asked our chum Fergal to come with us. He needed cheering up. He'd fallen in love at the last port, and couldn't forget his girl. We reckoned that if something happened two of us could stay together while the third fetched help. Also Fergal's strong shoulders would be useful. Eddie thought we should drag a pile of food around the nearest hill and hide it under a rock. It took all of one day, but Fergal was a good dragger. Now we had an emergency supply of food in case we needed it on the way back. None of us fancied being hungry. Not in such a cold, wild place.

Next day was blowing hard with drifting snow so we laid up and rested, and ate as much as we could. No point fussing about delays, Kettles taught us that. The wind and the weather ruled in this Land, and we must learn to go with it.

The day after was fine, so we started. We planned to walk around the hill, out over the frozen icy surface of the sea, to an island rising up in the distance. It shouldn't take too long, and once there we could climb to the top and get a view of what lay ahead.

We watched constantly for skuas with their harsh

screams. The skuas usually hung around the ship, grabbing food with their strong beaks. The Hefties were a wasteful lot and we hoped their piles of rubbish would keep the skuas occupied.

Near the rock where we had hidden our emergency food we found a dead skua chick in a stone nest. An excellent meal to get us on our way. We felt excited and proud. But solemn. Then we set off across the white frozen sea, walking one behind the other.

A narrow strip of open water glinted to our left. Suddenly an enormous black and white head reared out of the water, with glittering eyes. It swayed horribly from side to side staring in our direction.

'What *is* it?' whispered Fergal. We flattened ourselves along the ice. The head disappeared below the water with a sucking sound. We stayed still, not daring to move, until the cold crept into our beings and we had to get moving again. But all the time we cast worried glances back to the open water, fearing to see that monstrous head with its searching eyes.

We walked, we walked, and the island never got any closer. A curious grey-coloured cloud, low and long, hung in the distance. We wished it would go away. It was somehow frightening.

The cloud came towards us over the ice, slowly, silent, but never pausing, blotting out everything behind. Then it was upon us and a cruel, whipping wind attacked, filled with biting, stinging snow. The snow wasn't normal. It was like fine powder, or frozen dust, or needle-sharp grit. It hurt our eyes, stuck our lids together, caked our

fur. Now we were surrounded by greyness. We couldn't see the way ahead but we struggled on, stumbling over hidden ridges we didn't know were there.

Our ears and tails were so cold we'd stopped feeling them. Our whiskers were frozen to our faces. Our jaws were rigid. We couldn't keep going. With our last strength we pushed a pile of snow into a heap and burrowed inside, huddling our bodies tight around each other for warmth. Advice from Pedro, and life-saving. Slowly the snow melted from our fur into a puddle and we slept, out there on the frozen sea.

In the morning the sun shone brilliantly and we felt better. But where the cold had bitten our ears and tails they were swollen and throbbed with pain.

We trudged on across the frozen sea towards the island which seemed no closer. That's how the light worked in this place. You couldn't tell distances. But at last we reached the island. Our urgent need was food. Eddie found a few eggs scattered in a penguin nesting place. They were old, and frozen, but as all rats are taught by their mothers, any egg is better than no egg.

I began digging in the gritty gravelly earth. We had to

make homes here in this new Land, and I thought tunnels were probably the answer. But, only the depth of my body below the surface, I hit hardness. My claws scrabbled but nothing shifted. The earth was cold. As cold as ice. This earth was frozen solid. So that was the end of my tunnel idea. We were so weary we just lay down amongst the rocks and slept.

Next morning we started to climb the nearest hill, slipping on icy slopes, sharp stones cutting our feet. At last the three of us stood panting on the highest point.

There, to the south, was the same white level icy nothingness Eddie and I had seen from the balloon. A silent white world, glittering dully. Not an encouraging view to us explorers.

Scrambling and sliding down, we scavenged some more addled frozen penguin eggs, then set off on the long, long trek back across the sea ice to home. No eager steps, but a weary worn plod, plod. Now home was the place which never seemed to get any nearer. The wind whistled relentlessly across the ice, chilling us to our marrows. We made a snow heap and huddled inside it, for a miserable shivering sleep.

Next morning we set off again. Horribly hungry. Our legs aching with weariness. At last we reached the rock where we had hidden our food and scrabbled urgently. Oh, the deliciousness of that food! Now there was only a long trudge back to the ship, report to The Commander, huge dinner, and sleep in our comfortable nests.

We'd thought that travelling in this place meant

just travelling. It didn't. Unknown, unexpected dangers could happen at any moment, without warning. And everywhere was much further away than it looked, and more exhausting to reach. We had much to learn.

TWELVE

The Hefty huts were finished. They hunched on the dark pebbly ground, now newly streaked with snow, facing the frigid winds. But something wasn't right. Pedro had checked inside the biggest hut. It was stark, bare. It wouldn't do for a home for us rats at all. A winter in there would be the death of us. And there was hardly any food. The small Hefty huts were no use either – there wasn't a scrap of food in them. Goodness knows what they were for, said Pedro.

The Hefties were the other big puzzle. They were still on the ship, showing no proper signs of moving out. They weren't getting on with things. They kicked a ball around on the ice, and slid down snow slopes on wooden crates, or on pieces of wood which The Pilot said were skis.

Still The Commander hadn't announced the list of Stayers. We Volunteers had got to know each other pretty well by now. We'd welded ourselves into groups. So we worried a lot. Would The Commander keep our groups together, or would we be split up? Because the Stayers would be for ever different. For ever elite.

Suddenly The Commander called us to a Briefing and announced a new exploring party. A big one, this time. Rats rushed to be included. The Commander couldn't go because he'd wrenched his knee slipping on the ice. Pedro and The Pilot said openly that none of us knew enough about this place yet to risk another expedition. But The Commander insisted. We'd only find out by doing, he said.

The exploring party set off in single file at midnight. Ten fit rats running bravely across the snow. The sun set a couple of hours a night now, and the darkness helped with secrecy.

We who stayed behind ate far too much. The Hefties scoffed enormous meals. We could always pick and choose amongst their leftovers, and the Hefty cook wasn't the cleanest, so the galley was a haven of permanent scavenging.

A week after the exploring party left, an enormous storm shook the ship. We hoped that the exploring party were safely tucked into shelter. But at the storm's height four exhausted rats staggered on to the ship. Frozen. Gabbling nonsense. Their eyes staring. Gradually we got them to speak.

Exploring had been far tougher than they'd ever expected. They'd sunk in deep snow and cut their feet on frozen rocks. It had been cold. Terribly cold. They couldn't find enough to eat. The decision was made to return.

Then the storm had begun. They hid under boulders but they were shivering and hungry. They thought the ship was near. They decided to set out, even though they could hardly see in the whirling snow. Almost immediately they lost Jumper. They formed a line, each rat holding the tail of the one in front, to sweep the ground looking for him. In the confusing grey wildness of the storm they seemed to be on an icy slope. The slope got steeper. The rat in the lead started slipping. He managed to throw himself back, digging in his claws. So did the others. Except for one, Victor. Horrified, they saw him slide past, scrabbling desperately, and disappear. They tried going after him. But in four steps they found themselves on the edge of a terrible drop. Below, through the whirling snow, they saw the sea. They managed to scrabble and cling their way back up the slope. Somehow, they didn't know how, they got back to the ship.

It was a terrible story. Four of our number were safe. Two were missing. Four were yet to return.

Grim-faced, The Commander spoke to us all. 'We have been foolish and ignorant. None of us should have set out. We do not know enough about how to survive in this place. Searching for our companions now will only risk more lives. We can do nothing until the storm is over. We can only hope that our brave friends will come home, safely, and soon.'

The waiting was unbearable. Eddie and Kettles made nests for the four frozen rats who had returned, and gave them warm food. Eddie checked their cut feet, their frostbitten ears and tails. Kettles prepared nests and food for any other survivors. Then, thanks be, four rats stumbled in, all badly frostbitten. But still we were missing two.

Next morning the storm was over. That's what storms were like here. Blow up with no warning, violent, wild, then suddenly finish. The Pilot and Kettles went to the place where poor Victor had slipped. They peered over the edge. Far below, the sea dashed on rocks and ice. He hadn't a chance.

We were a heartbroken band of rats. We had lost two companions. This Unknown Land had taken two of us, so soon.

Next day a rat was seen wandering in a peculiar way, in the distance. The Pilot and Kettles dashed out. No one had permission to be on his own in this dangerous place. But it was Jumper.

We could not believe it. It was as if Jumper had come back from the dead. Eddie covered him gently with shredded wool, and fed him soft bread. He slept, and slept, and when he woke up he told us the most extraordinary story. He had lost everyone in the storm. So, feeling very tired, he lay down in the snow to sleep. The next thing he knew he woke up, very stiff, in a kind of bright cave. The cave was made of snow, which had piled over him. So he pushed out of the snow cave and wandered around.

Jumper had slept two nights and a day in the snow. He seemed none the worse for his amazing adventure. But poor Victor was dead.

THIRTEEN

The sun rolled around the horizon in a strange way and orange-red sunsets lasted for hours and hours. Sometimes we woke in the morning to find the water of our small bay covered in ice, a thin but solid sheet, and we fretted, and worried, because still our ship had not left. Then the wind blew and the ice broke into pieces and floated away, like bits of broken white paving. Each of us was ready to move on to the land at a moment's notice. And each steeled himself to be ordered to depart with the ship, to go from this place without doing what he had come to do.

'We must be patient,' said The Pilot. 'Whatever happens will happen.'

'Being The Commander is hard,' said Kettles. 'This Land makes its own rules and none of us understands them.'

But now The Commander made up his mind. He named the names. There were two lists. The Stayers. The Leavers. The waiting was over. The Stayers would move into the big hut ahead of the Hefties, establishing safe places to live. All of us were to work night and day to move supplies of food into the hut because the Hefties hadn't taken enough across.

Eddie was on the list of Stayers. I was a Leaver.

My disappointment was bitter. It bored into my heart like an icy needle, it thudded in my head. I was being sent away. It seemed like failure. I hadn't really begun to do the work I had come to do. I would go home, to gnaw at my discontent. I would have to live with the memory of what I could have done, what I did not do.

Eddie felt awful. 'It's because I'm medical,' he said. 'That's why I've been chosen.'

But we weren't given time to brood. Biter and Shaver began organising the Food Chain. Work started immediately.

My job was in the hold. I knew the Hefty food supplies well and I threw myself at the bags and boxes, trying to forget my pain by work. Dried minced beef, bacon rations, salt pork, barley, cabin biscuits, concentrated soup, preserved potatoes, carrots – I selected and sorted. Butter and margarine – we must have fat – treats like lump sugar, raisins, chocolate and apple rings, cheese of course. No fish because it only came in tins, there was some dried fish but I rejected the mouldy stuff. No grog – we couldn't carry it. Tobacco to chew in emergencies. I only chose easily transported food. Getting it across to the hut would be difficult enough.

The food piled up in a depot near the bow. Now the Food Chain swung into action. A spaced out line of Volunteers reached from the hold to the hut. Each hiding, yet each braving all to move the food. Rat number one moved a portion of food to number two, who moved it on, and so the food travelled, up ladders, along the deck, down the gangplank, across the sea ice, on to the land, past the dog kennels, and up to the hut. A risky, dangerous route. The food moved along the food chain in fits and starts; carried with pounding hearts, in fear, in boldness and exhaustion, and heroic unmarked deeds.

At the big bare hut Kettles and Pedro were in charge of gangs of gnawers and diggers. Hidden holes were made leading down to cold cramped spaces beneath the floorboards, the only safe place to store the food. Nature's blooming refrigerator again, said Jonas grimly. There was nowhere to build nests in that draughty empty hut. On land we ships' rats like living high up in buildings if we can, rafters, attics, inside walls, that kind of thing. But there was nowhere like that in the hut. So the Stayers would have to live on the ice-cold ground under the floor, where the food was stored. Once the Hefties move in we might find somewhere better, said Pedro. Pedro was a Stayer of course. But he sounded doubtful. Everyone tried to make the best of an unpleasant reality.

The hut was ready for the Stayers to move into

remarkably quickly. The Commander organised a party on the ship. But it was more like a wake. How could we celebrate? No one's heart was really in it. The Stayers were pleased and proud to be staying, but how could they show it without paining us Leavers? Yet already the Stayers were forming their own new group, breaking old friendships. That's the way it had to be, shared experience welding the group together, the shared anticipation of adventures ahead giving them private jokes, special words only they used.

The party dragged on. Some of us drank too much. Then we all stood to sing the Ships' Rat Song and the Stayers left the ship. For good.

But it was a bit of an anti-climax. The Hefties were still on board. The Commander remained on board, although of course he had chosen himself as a Stayer. And we Leavers did not know *when* we were leaving.

FOURTEEN

Winter was coming. We didn't need Pedro to tell us. The wind blew ever colder. No one wanted to be outside much. The last of the penguins walked away across the ice, squawking mournfully. Now even the last of the skuas left. The ice sighed and crunched. The seals stayed, but mostly under water. Outside, the world was wide and wild, white snow, black rock.

When would the ship go?

One evening as ice formed around our ship's hull, yet again, and the wind howled outside, The Commander called a Briefing. The Stayers slipped over from the hut to join us Leavers. We were a different-looking band of rats now. We were weather-beaten. Some had scars from frost-bites. Our coats were much, much thicker. They made us feel proud.

'I wish to announce that the plans have changed,' said The Commander.

'We were wondering,' murmured The Pilot.

'The Hefties appear not to be moving into their huts. Our ship does not appear to be departing. It seems that the Hefties will remain on board and spend the winter here. The Stayers therefore can abandon their quarters in the hut.

'All Volunteers will now live here on board. I need not tell you how comfortable we will be on this ship which we know so well.'

We all cheered, and cheered, until we were hoarse.

The Commander looked really happy. He indicated three large pannikins of rum. 'Let us drink to our new Winter Quarters!'

There was no more mention of dividing us band of Volunteers. We were all in this together.

> The best laid plans
> of rats and men
> depend on the wind and the weather,

hummed The Pilot and Kettles, grinning,

> When the blizzards blow,
> and there's ice and snow,
> we'll all live here together!

and they went off, arm in arm.

Eddie settled back on board with relief. 'That hut

was appallingly gloomy and uncomfortable,' was all he would say.

The next day a new layer of ice surrounded the ship. The Hefties stretched a canvas awning over the deck. Underneath, it was a bit like being in a tent. They began dismantling the engine and the boilers.

Almost immediately, much to our surprise, Hefties left on an expedition of their own. Their sledges were piled high with bundles. 'Everything on top and nothing handy,' said The Pilot, but he and The Commander slipped in amongst the bags and went with them. The Hefties harnessed dogs to their sledges as well as themselves, to help pull the heavy loads. None of us fancied being out on the ice with those terrible dogs. The Commander and The Pilot were very brave.

We were glad to see the sledges come back after only three days. The cold had been appalling, The Pilot told us, in a midnight session round the galley stove. The Hefties had groaned and shivered. Their expedition had been a bit of a failure. It was better to stay put, us rats and Hefties, each in our own parts of the ship. We knew how to manage that.

Three weeks later the sun disappeared. It did not rise. It did not set. All colour drained from our world. Darkness descended except for a kind of glow at midday. Winter was upon us.

Our ship was moored close to the shore. Now, as the sea froze, she no longer moved with the swell. She had ceased to be a living thing.

We were on our own. We were cut off completely

from the rest of the world. No news could reach us. No one could help us. We could not escape.

FIFTEEN

Inside, the ship was cold and damp. A layer of frost covered anything metal. Parts fugged up with heat from the stoves but move away and the air was icy. Water lying on the floors froze immediately into slippery sheets. The bilge water froze and a deep layer of grey ice filled the bottom of the hold. But we didn't mind the cold so much. Our thick fur coats saw to that. In fact we didn't like being too warm.

After our adventure with the wicker basket Eddie and I had moved into a Hefty's cabin and made a nest under his bunk. It was a nice enough home. Very crowded with his things, but cosy, with a constant edge of danger to keep us alert. Now bulging ice grew on the cabin wall, and icicles hung behind the drawers where he kept his clothes. An awful smell of mould made things unbearable. We needed somewhere new. Any old fool can be uncomfortable, as my grandmother used to say.

Our Hefty often went down into the hold. I tracked him and discovered that he and another Hefty had made themselves a hidden home with packing case walls and a door down a packing case passage which no one could get in, unless they let them. Cunning Hefties! Here they spent hours and hours. The packing cases were filled with raisins and chocolates. Eddie was delighted, and we moved in.

The sea–ice grew thicker. The ship shifted a little inside its ice prison, groaning, creaking, moaning. On freezing nights we sometimes heard ice cracking in the distance like pistol shots – very scary, until Pedro told us what it was. Sometimes we could hear seals swimming beneath the ship, calling to each other with whines and whistles and gurgling sounds that rose and fell almost like songs. Strange to think of the water beneath us. Mostly we forgot about it.

The Hefties lit their spaces with lamps and candles. Some worked at a big table cutting up penguins, and fish, which made a dreadful stink. Most nights a Hefty played the piano. We liked that. Ships' rats have a special fondness for music, but the same tunes, over and over, got very tedious.

A stationary ship meant idle Hefties. We were sure that they never suspected our presence. Not here in the Unknown Land. They were certainly easier to avoid now

74

they had so little to do. A few of us lurked behind the curtains to their cabins, or inside their clothes which were always draped around to dry, to pick up bits of food. We weren't hungry. Just bored. Some Hefties always slept after lunch, lying stretched out on tables or the floor. We played hide and seek around their snoring bodies, till we got bored with that as well. Our Sea Orders of course had been suspended, and there were no watch duties. The Commander tried to keep up the discipline of Ships' Rats' Rules. But it was difficult. It was too easy to be idle.

Very occasionally some of us went outside, into the bitter pinching cold, the lung-crunching air. It was dark, always dark, except for the pale thin light from the stars, or when the distant volcano belched out puffs of dull red smoke. Fire and ice. Ice and fire. How eerie it was living near that great volcano with its hidden glowing heart.

Outside, in the dark, you could begin to imagine things. To hear strange, weird noises. Or think you heard footsteps, and whip around – to nothing. Sometimes the silence was so loud it almost hurt, and you strained your ears to hear something – anything. It was easy to panic and most of us did, rushing back on board, to the black ship in the white immensity which was our home.

The wind blew almost non-stop, wailing through the rigging, stirring up the gritty snow. Even crossing the deck it stole the precious warmth from our bodies like a thief. We learned to keep out of the wind. We were lucky. Our bodies were already low to the ground.

The worst wind of all was a blizzard. 'If you are out when it blizzes,' Pedro warned, 'stay in one place or you'll be lost in an instant.' That's what happened to Lasher. He was only ten steps from the ship yet he wandered bewildered, numbed, with the blizzard's deafening roar in his ears. Whirling snow plastered his eyes, filled his nose and mouth. Just in time he stumbled across a rope the Hefties had strung from the ship to guide themselves in the dark, and grasping it felt his way back on board, his face a frozen mask of ice.

Extreme cold affected us. We became slow, foolish. Survival required being alert, on the watch, all senses functioning. The cold was a trap. It gave no warning. It gave no time. This Unknown Country was unforgiving.

Most of us curled up and slept a lot these strange winter days. A few of us used the chance for skags, long talks about life and our hopes, that kind of thing. Some rats grumbled. Some became gloomy, or started to hate the place, missing home, and love. We all got on each other's nerves, and sometimes there were angry arguments. Once or twice nasty fights broke out. Certain rats began to loathe each other but they moved to opposite ends of the ship. It's hard being cooped up for so long. We were getting irritable, discontented. And lazy. And fat. With our long thick hair we looked like walking fur coats.

None of us talked about the work that was to come. The winter had to be got through first.

When the wind howled and storms blew all was pitch black. The loss of the sun affected us deeply. It was as if something necessary to life had been taken away. It was difficult to know night from day, or one day from the next. After a while all days seemed to roll into one long night.

SIXTEEN

An immense blizzard began. The wind blew in furious gusts without stopping, howling and screeching in the rigging. To be on a ship in such a storm, yet not be moving. That was strange. I poked my head outside, just for a moment. The night was blacker than coal. The wind hammered, snow rushed at me, exploding against my face, clogging my nostrils, my mouth, blinding my eyes. The feeling was terrible. Like being suffocated by a fiendish monster, attacked by some implacable enemy.

After the blizzard our ship was smothered in white. Everything looked different. Great drifts of snow had piled up on the windward side higher than the deck – pure white hills with sculpted edges.

Inside the ship the dark days were rolling on always the same. But I was young, I needed to be doing something. It wasn't good for me to be moping around idle. It wasn't good for my teeth, either. I needed to keep gnawing and I wasn't bothering. And I was still worried about how we would find somewhere to live in this new country. All this, with the drifts, gave me my idea.

I called my own private meeting, by the starboard scuttle hatch. All was dark and dreary as usual. The wind whistled through the rigging. Thin powder snow drove across the deck. Eddie came of course, with Fergal, Skelly and Padders. I added Jonas, the cheerful rat who'd joined the ship at the last moment. I didn't ask Pedro, or Kettles, or The Pilot. They knew about Polar things, and I wanted this to be my idea. And I wanted it to be a secret. Six were enough.

I'd done some work first, though.

'Follow me,' I said proudly, and I took my mates off the ship, through a cunningly hidden hole, and *into the snow-drift*! I'd made ten solid snow steps, then dug a passage into the centre of the drift, ending in a small rounded chamber. It hadn't been difficult – hard work, but good gnawing. The walls were smooth and shiny, twinkling with ice crystals. I'd made chairs of ice, with arms, and comfortable backs. Even though it was dark outside, a kind of faint bluey light filtered through the snow.

My mates were amazed! I lounged back on my chair and grinned with pleasure. 'It's my idea,' I said. 'We can all dig a special home here in the snow-drift, somewhere

we can get away on our own. We can each make our own kind of room. We connect everything up, and it's all perfectly safe! No Hefties! No dogs! It's our secret. And who knows, this may be the way we can live here in this new Land, in years to come? We have to find out if we can do it.'

My mates gathered round and cheered. It was a brilliant idea. We all started gnawing at the ice right away, making new tunnels leading down from the upper chamber deeper into the great snow-drift. Each of us made a room to suit ourselves. Mine had arches, and cupboards, and a shelf to put my lucky piece of moss on. Eddie decorated his with beautiful fringes of icicles. Jonas decided to try sleeping in his room, unravelling some Hefty wool socks for a deep nest. Fergal's room had a secret space where he thought about his true love. Padders built exercise equipment – a bar made of ice to swing around, pebble weights to lift. Skelly made three rooms, constructing each on different principles.

We dug an escape hole. We always have more than one exit in our homes. No one wants to be caught like a rat in a trap. The snow-drift was warmer than we expected. It wasn't stuffy or draughty or damp or dirty like the ship. We called it 'The Ice Palace'.

Fergal had the idea of dragging some food supplies over from the ship. Getting them off without anyone noticing wasn't easy, and of course they froze, but it was a useful experiment.

Then Padders had an amazing idea. We were all sitting in the upper chamber, nibbling on Fergal's food supply. 'Let's give a party,' he said. 'A big wonderful wild middle-of-winter let everything rip party for everyone. We band of Volunteers need something special. It means sharing our secret, I know. But it will be worth it! We can block off the passages to our rooms so no one will find them. But let's gnaw out one enormous party room big enough to hold us all!'

Skelly stood up. 'I'm game,' he said, 'but on condition that I design it to make it safe.'

'I'll organise the music,' said Eddie.

'I'll plan the food,' said Fergal.

'I'll bring the grog,' said Jonas.

'And I'll arrange the entertainments,' I said.

So we started. The party room began to take shape, and it was a wonder. It was near the bottom of the snow-drift for safety, with an entrance tunnel, a separate exit tunnel, and two ingenious ventilation tunnels for fresh air, one low, one high up. Skelly instructed us to leave four thick snow pillars to support the vaulted ceiling, which sparkled and glinted with delicate ice crystals. Around three walls we made curving ice seats for sitting on and relaxing. The fourth wall had a wide ice stage with thrones for the Ice King and Ice Queen. In one corner was the bar made of clear ice, and in the opposite corner an ice table for the food. Last thing, we smoothed the floor ready for dancing.

Bit by bit Fergal had been collecting the food. What a feast! Eddie and I helped with the chocolate and raisins of course, but Fergal had worked his way into the cheese supply. His greatest prize was a Christmas pudding he'd found in the hold behind the bacon. Then there were currants, jellies, jams, a nice little pile of sardine bits, some ham, prunes, even a mutton bone. He planned to get fresh cakes on the day, removed with cunning from the Hefty cook.

I kept my entertainments a secret by arranging with certain rats to do something without telling them what it was for.

We asked The Commander for permission to have a party. He seemed happy to give it. The Pilot had been observing the Hefties and reckoned they were planning a feast the next night, so we chose that. Hefty feasts were always so noisy they wouldn't notice ours.

The night of the party everyone assembled in the Meeting Place in the hold. We'd dressed up a bit, with shredded string skirts, and wigs. We'd groomed our thick coats till they were glossy and gleaming. Some rats looked unhappy because they thought we were having the party in the hold and they couldn't see anything to eat. Up above, the Hefties had already begun their feast.

Then we led our fellow Volunteers in a long line

through the ship, across the deck, through the scuttle hatch, and into the silence and privacy of our secret home in the snow-drift. Their astonishment was wonderful. But nothing compared to the sight of our own beautiful glittering ice party room, table overflowing with food, bar filled with grog! As a final surprise Skelly had gnawed big pieces of clear ice into beautiful ice statues. There was a model of our ship, entwined hearts, and best of all a glorious female rat sitting on an anchor. Billy Stumps wept with joy.

First in came the Ice King and Ice Queen, Fergal and Eddie dressed up, but no one knew. The Ice King had a fine black wig and a crown of ice diamonds, and an icicle for a sceptre. The Ice Queen's long golden wig sparkled with a gold chain borrowed for the occasion from one of the Hefties. They sat on their thrones and the Ice King declared the party open.

What a party! Eddie played a clever instrument, a wire stretched over a tin, which he twanged. My entertainments went down a treat – songs, jokes, more songs, reciting poems – everyone was so happy, it didn't matter what they listened to. Pedro gave us a wonderful talk about his expedition, and The Commander seemed to really enjoy it. Kettles and The Pilot sang elaborate Polar songs. Lasher recited a dirge-like poem about the long dark winter – days upon days of darkness, the miserable sight of the long dark night with no chance for flight. But no one minded.

Then the dancing started. Jonas and Shaver had brought their instruments, just in case, and with Eddie leading, the music went faster and faster, while we whirled and sped around the polished ice floor, dancing in the way only ships' rats know how. Shouting, singing, dancing, drinking, stuffing down food – what a party! The noise was terrific, but deep inside our snow-drift nothing mattered – no one could hear us.

At midnight every one of us made the loudest noise he could, yelling, banging, thumping tails and feet. Jumper tried to start a snowball fight, but our ice walls were too hard and smooth.

Gradually the party slowed. Rats laid peacefully along the ice seats and snored. Others slumped by the table, food still within reach but stomachs full.

I'd composed a special song for the party, all about home, and absent friends, and us being at the end of the world; very romantic, and sentimental. I had a fine voice and it went down well.

Now the party was over. Eddie and I looked around at our sleeping companions, our wonderful handiwork, and the mess. I sang the chorus, softly.

> We're far from home
> in the land of snow.
> Our ship is moored
> by the great ice floe.
> But however far,
> we always know,
> That our loved ones wait.
> That our loved ones wait.

We are far from home, Eddie,' I said. 'A very, very

long way, and we are stuck here.'

'I know, Hackle,' said Eddie. 'I know.' And we both cried a little, to think of our dear Vanilla and Clemmy waiting for us.

SEVENTEEN

The Commander called Eddie and me into his private quarters, a neat gap between the wardroom and the inner sheathing of the hull. We were surprised. He didn't usually talk to anyone except Scouts. Recently he'd been even more secretive than usual, silent and withdrawn. He'd got a lot to worry about, at least that's what Eddie thought.

The Commander walked quickly across and back, across and back, like a trapped animal behind a door waiting for it to open.

'We have been able to survive here with no real hardship,' he said. 'We know we can live on Hefty ships wherever they are. But to really live in this Land –

to take it for our own – we must be able to live independently of all Hefties, all local humans. We have to find our own supplies of food. We have to find places where we can make our own homes. That is the goal for the months ahead. Once spring comes, parties will set out in different directions, with many tasks. We do not know how long the Hefties are staying here. We must be ready to go out and work at our tasks as soon as we can.'

He drummed his claws against the sheathing of the hull.

'But I,' he said. 'I am marching to a different tune.

'Our ship has come far to the south. The Great Ice Plain begins almost at our door. You both have seen it from the island; and from the balloon. We ships' rats know to use rivers as the routes inland. But here in this Unknown Land there are no rivers. Instead, there is ice.

'I have been thinking, deeply. The Great Ice Plain is like a frozen river. It stretches into the distance. It beckons me. It calls me south. I want to get further south than any rat. The furthest south in all the world is the South Pole. I must get there. I intend to be the first.'

The words came quickly. His eyes glittered. He seemed all energy, tight muscles tensed like a sail in a gale.

'A small party only will come with me. We must travel fast and light.'

He paused, then, circling us with quick, forceful steps, 'I have chosen you to be my companions,' he said. 'I am aware that my choice will be a surprise to you. You are of course not even Scouts. But I need you, Eddie, because of your medical knowledge. It may be wanted if an accident should occur. You, Hackle, are resourceful and enthusiastic, and Eddie and you are mates. We will need to be mates on such a journey.

'Our plans for the Southern Journey must remain a secret until I am ready to announce them.'

Eddie and I stood awkward, silent, completely astonished. We hardly knew what to think. A journey south? That wasn't why we had come here, to the Unknown Land. Yet – yet – something had taken The Commander, was sweeping him up, a kind of vision.

Suddenly I remembered the look on Pedro's face when he had come back from his trip on the Hefty sledge, at the place where the balloon was launched. He had said something strange. 'I got the furthest south.'

I hadn't understood him. Now I knew. Pedro had felt the call of the South Pole. He was a secret Pole-seeker. The Commander had become one as well. Perhaps that is what stood, shadowy, between them.

Eddie and I left The Commander's private quarters and went outside. Both of us needed to think. A huge moon hung like a bulging speckled ball in the black sky. It shone on the frozen sea and the snowy slopes of the hills. Its silvery light picked out the peaks and glaciers of the distant mountains. The dogs tethered to their kennels howled, one by one, an ordered baying to the moon which made our hair stand on end. But the dogs were outsiders, like us.

This Land filled me with a feeling of nothingness, of total insignificance. It was magnificent, desolate. It did not care if we chose to do something. It did not care if we left, or stayed, if we died, or struggled heroically.

'Can we do it, Hackle?' asked Eddie.

'We have to,' I replied. 'We have been chosen.'

'It is *the* long journey,' said Eddie.

We gazed up at the moon shining down with such uninterrupted clarity on this wild unknown world. The moon had shone through the windows of the Experimental Lighthouse the evening we heard Pedro talk. It would shine on our families and our dear loved ones in the great bustling city so far away. The moon seemed a link in a chain that held us to our other lives.

'Come and see something,' said Eddie. He led me inside the ship and climbed along the beam above the wardroom table. There, under the skylight, was a bowl of earth. Two flowers were growing, their delicate petals reaching up. It made my breath catch to see these reminders of home.

He didn't have to say it. We might never see a flower again, never feel grass under our feet, or see the flickering shadows of sun through leaves. We might never again hold our loved ones in our arms.

I turned away. 'Come,' I said. 'We must prepare as best we can.'

EIGHTEEN

Eddie and I began the SJFC – the Southern Journey Fitness Campaign. The SJFC was difficult to hide from our mates. We told them we were working on a surprise in The Ice Palace. A lie, but what could we do? We were sworn to secrecy.

The Commander gave us special permission to go off ship. We'd noticed that some Hefties went out every day whatever the conditions. Now we began following them, learning new routes, and survival skills, hardening ourselves.

We practised eating snow. On the ship we rats drank the water the Hefties made by melting ice over the stove. But there would be no water out on the Great Ice Plain.

Snow turned our mouths numb, and an awful lot of snow was needed for even a sip of water.

The SJFC's first major objective, we decided, would be an ascent of the Black Hill. It was some distance from the ship, but two Hefties often walked to it so we knew the way. The days were still dark, of course, and desperately cold, but we'd manage as long as the wind didn't get up. That meant waiting for a calm day.

The first steep snow slope was easily climbed. But the cold did nip our ears badly. Our fine big naked ears were always vulnerable. We rubbed them hard. It hurt, but done in time rubbing stopped the misery of frostbite. Then the bare tips of our noses got nipped. So we stopped and rubbed each other's; laughing, because we looked a bit silly. Up, up we went, over icy ridges, a long hard climb, to a flat area of snow and ice which began sloping upwards again.

Suddenly I was falling, tumbling. Then – crash! I stopped, my head stuck between lumps of ice, my legs in the air. All the breath knocked out of me. The snow had just given way beneath my feet. No warning. Just given way.

'Hackle! Hackle!' Eddie was leaning over the edge up above, calling down desperately.

'I'm all right,' I managed to call back. But I wasn't. I was terrified. My limbs felt stiff and numb. A silent, chilling coldness drained my body's warmth. I had to do something, now, while I had strength or I never would. Somehow I wriggled right way up and looked around.

I was inside the ice, in a kind of narrow split, or crack. Below me the crack went on down, into terrifying empty blackness. I began shaking with fear. I couldn't stop. This must be a crevasse. Pedro had warned us about them. The walls of the crack were shiny ice, bulging, solid. Above me the ice walls curved on up to the surface. I crouched on the ice lump which had saved me.

My heart was heavy with despair. I hadn't died in the fall. But now I would die a slow death from cold and hunger. In the end I would slip off and fall down into the dreadful depths.

'Hackle!' It was Eddie again, sounding far away. 'Try! Please try. For me. For Clemmy. For all of us.'

I roused myself. A little beyond where I was standing, the walls of the crack narrowed. I edged along, not daring to look down. If I leaned my back against one side of the crack and wriggled up, using my claws on the other side, as if I was getting up a narrow chimney back home – I might do it. I had to try. Wriggling, panting, desperate, I began working my way up the crack towards the distant open air. I'm a ships' rat. I'm a good climber. I'm a ships' rat. I can climb. I kept repeating the words, willing myself on.

The ice walls were milky smooth and slippery. I had to keep resting, then make myself begin again. Eddie's anxious face stared down. With one last effort I reached up, Eddie leaned over, grabbed me, and with a mighty heave I was out.

I lay on the snow exhausted. There had been no sign that this dreadful crack was waiting under the snow to swallow me up.

Eddie and I crept back down the hill to the ship.

In the quiet middle of the night Eddie woke me gently. Hefties always cooked themselves snacks over a little lamp when they came back to the ship. Toasted cheese. Fried sardines. The smell was entrancing. Eddie had managed to scavenge a bit for me. What a friend.

I stayed in bed for several days nursing my bruises and feeling truly sorry for myself. When it was time to get up I went outside. It was a night of absolute calm when the snow lay like a velvet pall over the land, and the eerie beauty of this place took hold.

Suddenly the sky began to glow. Curtains of shimmering light appeared, and hung in the darkness. The curtains were silver and palest gold, stretching up, up into the distant heights of the sky. They began moving, flowing, as curtains move if a gentle wind blows across their folds. But there was no sound at all. The night was absolutely silent, still. Fringes of green light appeared, flickering along the hem of the curtains. Then beams of green light shot up into the sky almost too fast to see, quivering, darting, pulsing up and retracting.

I lay on my back in the snow, marvelling. It was as if the grandest, most beautiful music was playing, too far away for hearing. Yet my soul could listen.

The shimmering curtains gradually dimmed, and withdrew. The sky was dark again. I went inside feeling humble, unimportant. I would never, could never, forget.

NINETEEN

There was a feeling in the air. Just a hint, but we knew that the sun was coming back. A line of brightness where Earth met sky became daily stronger and wider and glowed wonderful colours, the pinks and orange of sunrise, except the sun hadn't risen. It hadn't risen for more than one hundred days. Skelly had kept count.

'I think this is it,' said Pedro one day. 'Climb as high as you can, and wait.'

So we did. We faced the glowing horizon. And then we saw it. The whole sun. Its blessed yellow rays streamed out across the snow and touched our bodies. I can't describe how joyful we felt. Eddie and I danced, Skelly and Padders cheered, and Fergal wept. The sun climbed clear and round into the sky.

Every day the sun climbed a little higher, and stayed for longer. Everything seemed to pick up. Everyone seemed to have a new zest for life. The long dark night of winter was over, over! Spring was on its way.

The Commander called a Briefing. He announced the plans, from which so much was hoped. There would be short and long expeditions, investigations to find food, searches for places to live, wide-ranging attempts to discover the animals and any local humans that lived here. The Volunteers had much to do.

Eddie and I hated keeping the Southern Journey from our mates. We hoped the secrecy would now be over. It was. The Commander paused. No one knew the size of this Unknown Land, he said. No one knew where the South Pole even was. It was his duty to find it, if he could, and get there, on behalf of all ships' rats.

I saw Pedro's tail twitching from side to side in an agitated way, and The Pilot pulling at his whiskers grimly. I was right. Pole-seeking was deep in Pedro's heart. But I had not thought that The Pilot also felt its power.

Our mates were very proud of Eddie and me for being chosen. And a bit awed. Some of the Scouts were jealous. I don't blame them. The Pilot and Pedro kept their mouths tight shut.

We celebrated in The Ice Palace, with a humdinger feast, our mates and us. They teased us, and said we would be famous. Skelly and Padders had been thinking of forming a band of explorers, and offering its services to The Commander. Skelly wanted to call it the Guarantee

Party – go anywhere and do anything. They were sad we couldn't join. But we sat around all night planning what it could do, and where it could go.

I'd been worrying hugely about food on the Southern Journey. I didn't know how we were going to eat out on the Great Ice Plain. The Hefties dragged their food on sledges. But what could we do? I reckoned that this Unknown Land had food around the edges. Penguins nested on the edges, seals lived there, and birds. Fish and other good things lived in the sea. But The Commander wanted us to go south. That meant going inland, away from the sea. What could live on the Great Ice Plain? Nothing could grow on ice, so nothing *could* live there. So there would be nothing to eat.

'You're right, Hackle,' said Skelly. 'All the expeditions The Commander has planned are along the edges. The Guarantee Party can live off the land.' He shook his head. 'I don't know what you will do.'

But I shouldn't have worried. The Commander had thought of a plan. We would carry our food. He'd got hold of some special Hefty expedition supplies. Lightweight and nutritious, he said. They looked pretty unappetising and tasted worse. Powders, meat ground up and mixed with fat, squares of soup and bacon. The only good thing was a thick hard biscuit, delicious and strangely filling.

Eddie and I were ordered to scavenge the food bags Hefties used for storing sugar and pack them full of Hefty expedition food. We would drag the bags behind us, said The Commander, gripping the draw cords in our teeth.

I wasn't convinced. How could we drag enough? But you didn't argue with The Commander.

TWENTY

The sun might be shining but it had no warmth. We still needed every hair of our thick long coats. Then one morning after a terrific storm Biter came rushing back to the ship with the astonishing news that there was open sea at the head of the bay. The ice had broken into pieces and floated away.

All our plans were thrown into confusion. It was as if a road had suddenly opened to our route home. Our ship was still frozen in its icy prison of course. But now the possibility of escape was there. Some time – soon – the rest of the ice would break away and we would be free to leave. Free! Billy Stumps and Snatcher found the rum and sang songs about their girls in every port. The winter had been long and hard for everyone. Fergal couldn't stop smiling. Surely all expeditions would be cancelled now? Surely our ship would leave as soon as it could?

But next day The Commander summoned Eddie and me. 'The Hefties are about to depart on their first expedition of spring,' he said briskly. 'I am certain the ship will not leave without them. It is imperative that we three accompany the Hefties. I must, and you both need the experience.'

I was appalled. I had no desire in the whole world to go near a Hefty sledge, or their terrible dogs. But The Commander was already over the side of the ship and checking the waiting sledges. A mean, biting wind gusting out of a flat grey sky flapped at the canvas coverings. Stinging gritty snow piled against the runners.

'Now,' ordered The Commander, and leaped on to a sledge. Eddie and I had to follow. We worked our way down amongst the packages just as the Hefties arrived with the dogs. We lay between a rolled-up sleeping bag and food boxes, listening to the growling and whining of the excited animals as they were harnessed to the traces. Whips cracked, Hefties shouted, and the sledges began lurching and slipping across the ice.

The sensation was horrible. Each bump and tip, each stumble and jerk, couldn't be anticipated, because we couldn't see anything. Once our sledge turned over with a dreadful thud but we were jammed too tight to move.

At last the sledges stopped. 'Get deeper,' hissed The Commander. 'They'll only unpack the first layer.' I eat when I'm worried. So I gnawed a corner of the sleeping bag. Small comfort, but better than nothing.

Our luck held. The Hefties dragged clumsily at their bundles in the freezing wind. We made ourselves comfortable enough, broke into the Hefty food, and soon were happily eating expedition grub. It was good to have a chance to know The Commander a bit better.

Next morning the Hefties pushed their things back on the sledge. I looked out and felt the wind hit, metal cold. Poor Hefties, out in that. On we went, all day, who knew where. By the time the Hefties pitched camp half a blizzard was blowing.

We'd decided to wait until the middle of the night to explore. Climbing out of our cramped quarters, we found that the wind had dropped. The sky glittered like an enormous black upturned bowl encrusted with millions of bits of broken mirror.

The Hefties were camped in a valley of broken, twisted ice, with ice cliffs either side, split and splintered as if by lightning. The silence was absolute. The cold was intense.

Almost immediately I tripped into a crack, bruising my leg. It was no good. In this land we were always living on the edge of managing. Stop concentrating for one moment, and the place would get you. We started back for the sledges. Perhaps the cold was already affecting my judgement, but stupidly I went too close to a dog lying curled in the snow. The great brute leaped up growling, its yellow eyes glaring. The other dogs started yowling. We ran back to our sledge, my leg in pain, but no matter; we had to move.

Thank the Great Rat, the dogs were chained and couldn't follow. But they could reach each other and they started fighting furiously. The Hefties stumbled out of their tents and dragged the dogs off each other. We three rats tucked down in our sledge and had a good feed of expedition biscuit. Nothing like a near escape to sharpen the appetite.

The Commander found a place where we could peer out the side of the sledge. So all next day, bracing ourselves against every jolt, we watched the twisted ice cliffs, riddled with caves, pass by. Snow began falling. A perishingly cold wind blew. The cliffs seemed to be part of a long snout of ice which tumbled in frozen motion from the land to where the sea would be, if it hadn't been covered in ice.

Next day the sun shone bright. Tiny glittering snow crystals fell silently from a clear blue sky. The Hefties set off climbing over the ice cliffs so we slipped away for a bit of quick exploring.

As we ran along the edge of the ice cliffs I began to hear a familiar sound, a sound that wrenched at my heart. I lifted my nose. There. I could smell it. It *was* the sea. The sound of waves, the smell of the salt ocean! We sped towards it. And there was moving water. The run and curve of waves. We had come to the place at the head of the bay where the ice had broken out.

We got amongst some penguins. They squawked, and flapped their stubby wings, and pushed each other nearer and nearer the water as if wanting to go in, but not wanting to be first. We three lay gazing at the sea and listening to the good familiar sucking and slapping of water against the ice.

Then we heard a new noise. A deep rasping breath. We peered over the ice edge – straight at the huge snake-like head and spotted chest of a seal. This wasn't the kind of seal that lay around dozing on the ice. It was dangerous-looking, an ugly brute, all wide gaping jaws and sharp teeth. It curved its great back and slipped quietly beneath the surface.

The Commander dragged us away from the ice edge. 'I don't like it and I don't trust it,' he muttered. Suddenly the seal launched itself out of the water, jaws snapping, huge body half up on the ice where we had been lying. The penguins scattered in terror. The seal sank back heavily into the water. We ran and didn't stop until we were back at the camp.

We arrived just before the Hefties. They ate, struck camp, and we were off again in the sledges. Fast, this time. We were resting after our fright, not watching where we were going. Suddenly our sledge crashed to a standstill. Terrifying snarling and howling started right by our ears. Our hair stood on end. The dogs were fighting on top of the sledge! Surely they would smell us! Hefties shouted and cracked their whips. The sledge rocked, the dogs growled and fought.

Slowly things calmed. Our sledge started again. Exhausted, we slept, and didn't wake up till the sledges stopped. The Commander peered cautiously out. 'By the Great Thunderer, we're back at the ship!' he exclaimed.

Eddie and I were very glad. It was good to be in the warmth of our quarters, get clean, meet with our mates behind the galley stove over a good bit of grub, and tell our adventures.

'It's just as well you moved from the ice edge,' said Pedro. 'That seal would have had you for breakfast, never mind your furry coats!'

TWENTY-ONE

Now a new tragedy struck our small band of Volunteers. We were certain that the Hefties had never seen us, never guessed that we shared their quarters. But the dogs: they were something different.

A few dogs had broken loose and the appalling animals ranged over the ice seeking out seals and killing them. I suppose we were getting too confident. With the return of the sun, rules were being broken. Rats were going off without permission. That was how the tragedy happened. Shaver and Dundee went to check out the big Hefty hut. But only Shaver came back. He wouldn't talk about what happened, but we knew it must have been a dog. 'Just one snap of the jaws, that's all it needs,' said Tankey, who liked talking about tragedies.

After the death of Dundee, The Commander imposed strict discipline. The Scouts patrolled, orders were given, there was no leaving the ship without permission. We were here to do a job and for no other reason.

We were flabby, said The Commander. Start eating properly, exercise more, sleep less. Eddie and I, of course, were fit from the SJFC. But that was our secret. Fighting competitions were organised to get us in trim. The fights were strictly controlled. No one wanted any accidents.

In spite of the distant open sea, the Hefties continued to leave on expeditions. We couldn't understand it. But they vastly improved the method of sledge packing and there was simply no space to squeeze a rat in. So none of us went. The weather was still horribly cold. Blizzards blew in with no warning. The Hefties came back thin, miserable, with frostbitten cheeks and fingers, some of them ill.

The Commander decided that our expeditions had to get started as well, and several were sent out. But our mates came back like the Hefties, frostbitten, miserable, some ill. The bare skin of our ears and noses, paws and feet had toughened and thickened during our time in this land. But we couldn't stand being out too long in this desperate cold.

Then the ice came back over the sea at the head of our bay. So that was that: our ship couldn't move.

Yet the days were very gradually getting warmer. The canvas awning over the ship's deck was taken down and the spring sun showed the mess and muddle, the blackness and filth – even for us rats, it was a bit much. In the unexpected light we looked unhealthy, as if we'd lived for months in a city cellar and never seen the sun; which is after all what the winter had been like. Hefties started cleaning, shifting things around. The wardroom looked like old Ma Bootle's wash house in Lower Wharf Street back home, wet Hefty clothes draped everywhere over washing lines.

One morning we watched some immense penguins walking solemnly one behind the other on their big horny feet, beaks lifted imperiously, their lemony-white fronts glowing in the sun. 'Do you see where they're going?' said Fergal. 'They're going *south*. That must mean there's something worth having there.' Eddie and I felt a bit encouraged.

Now spring was definitely here. All over the ship water trickled. Long winter icicles began dripping. The frozen bilge-water in the hold melted and smelt foul. The ship stank of mould. With all the sorting and shifting Eddie and I moved with our mates into the snow-drift. But now our Ice Palace began melting. Drips splashed from the ceilings. Tunnels collapsed. Passages became slush. Our splendid home was turning into a humble pond. I was terribly disappointed. My great idea had proved a failure.

We missed our beautiful Ice Palace, deeply. We missed our private spaces, our peace. We mourned our memories. We'd had such good times in it. But now we knew that snow-drifts were no use for year-round living. We would have to find permanent homes somewhere else if we were going to stay in this new Land.

Some of us had been put on Egg Patrol checking the penguins. The penguins were building their pebble nests. Crafty thieves, they were always stealing each other's pebbles. We tried stealing pebbles for the fun of it, but we didn't want them. We wanted penguin eggs. What a feast that would be!

The skuas were back, as big and hungry as ever. They swooped around the penguins, checking future dinners. Rats and skuas. Soon we'd be competing for the same food. There was enough for all, but we didn't know who would come off better in a fight.

We found out, soon enough. One of our strongest Scouts, Cruncher, was searching through the penguin nesting place greedy for the first fresh egg when a skua attacked him from behind. Cruncher whipped around and bit the skua on the leg. The skua arched its neck and screamed and pecked, Cruncher scratched and bit, hissing, tail lashing, until both limped off wounded. One all, but no one was keen to try another fight. We would have to watch out, all the time.

The Commander had chosen our friends in the Guarantee Party to explore the coast. Rats would only ever be able to live along the coast, we reckoned, and we needed to find the best places. No one saw the Guarantee Party go. That was typical. No fuss, just slip away. They came back ten days later ravenously hungry. There wasn't much to encourage us in their report. Almost no land had been found free of ice and snow. Any that was bristled with nesting penguins.

The Land was generally buzzing with life again. But

Kettles wisely pointed out that all the animals we'd so far found depended on the sea. That's where they got their food. Or they ate the things that got their food in the sea. We rats can swim a bit. We like fish, but we couldn't go into the sea and get fish. We're happy to eat eggs and birds but they were seasonal. We needed more. We hadn't found any grasses or seeds growing yet, any fruits, nuts or vegetables. And we needed to be able to store supplies for the long winter, the time of dearth.

All this had been Pedro's experience. But he'd only done the briefest bit of exploring. He'd hoped that he'd been unlucky, and hadn't been in the right parts.

The Commander ordered the Scouts to take penguin eggs and hide them in a special cache for next winter. Dangerous work, what with the patrolling skuas, and the Hefties stealing eggs as well.

But underneath, we were all wondering about our future in this place.

TWENTY-TWO

The time came for our own expedition, the Southern Journey.

The Journey was waiting for us like a beckoning presence. It sat, just beyond the horizon. I felt powerless. It had to be done. Not one of us knew where the South Pole was, or what it was, or whether it could ever be reached. It seemed to be a place of silence, of uncertainty, of unnamed, unknowable terrors. But The Commander was like a rat possessed. The other expeditions happened. Our expedition was all he lived for.

Like a machine, The Commander planned and calculated. Everything depended on food. We could do nothing without it. So Advance Parties were sent out, dragging food supplies for us to use along the route. We needed food on the way to the South Pole. But we needed food on the way back as well. The Advance Parties led by Pedro and The Pilot travelled seven days before burying the food supplies in the First Depot. In so doing they explored the beginnings of the route: out across the sea ice and on to the Great Ice Plain, the highway that led to the south. Several times they had been beaten back by desperate cold and bitter winds. Their work had been hard.

The sun now set only during the middle hours of the night. Yet still we waited for better weather. Waiting was hard. We were ready to go at a moment's notice. Then another blizzard would blow in, making it impossible to start. The weather ruled in this Land. We understood that now.

The message came from The Commander late on a raw grey day when the wind drove newly revealed grit along the ground like small hard weapons. We were to leave at midnight. The area round the ship was busy with Hefties and this was the safest moment.

I spent the first part of the evening with my particular mates talking about old times. I asked Fergal to tell Clemmy that I loved her, if I never came back from the Southern Journey. And to tell her that I had gone on the Journey for the honour of all rats, and she must be proud of me. Eddie left the same kind of message for his dear Vanilla.

We gathered for a farewell feast. I didn't feel much like eating, even though there was my favourite seal pie, and sardines, and fresh cakes baked by the Hefty cook.

Our Expedition was toasted by all the Volunteers with a special toast for the Southern Journey, 'Hope on, hope ever.'

We sang the Ships' Rat Song. Eddie had planned a new chorus for the occasion.

> We are the ships' rats. Ships' rats are we.
> Frostbitten, snow-blind, hardened and free.
> Bravely travelling the New Country.
> Exploring together!
> Ships' rats forever!

The Commander had left orders. He'd divided the Volunteers again into a small group of Stayers and a larger number of Leavers. If the ship departed before we returned the Leavers would go with it. The Stayers were to move into the big hut where we would join them when we got back. At least I was a Stayer now.

The Pilot was the last to shake my hand. He wanted to be with us on the Southern Journey. I knew that. Instead he had been left in charge of everything. 'The long trail, the hard trail, the dark trail lies ahead,' he said. 'I wish you all the luck you'll need.'

Our companions climbed silently up the rigging and clung on in neat respectful lines, giving us an honourable farewell, each holding out a clenched fist, true ships' rat style.

The Commander, Eddie and I stood on the snow gazing up at the rigging, at all our good friends, the band of Volunteers. The squally wind was still gusting bits of grit. It was a mean, distrustful wind. My heart felt as if it would burst. I was proud to be going. But also filled with the uncertainty of all that lay ahead.

'This is our home,' said Eddie softly, to me. 'This is the centre of our lives. We are going we know not where, to do we know not what.'

'Come,' said The Commander. 'The South Pole! Think of it!'

We each had a food bag filled, and heavy. At the bottom of mine I had hidden my piece of lucky moss, the only thing I had ever found growing in this country. We waved our last farewell. Then we gripped the draw cords of our food bags in our teeth and started out across the ice, hauling. We would see a land that no rats had ever seen before.

TWENTY-THREE

As soon as I left the ship I felt better. Getting away was the hard bit.

The Commander had our expedition all planned, using a very clever method. He'd had the idea of dividing our journey up into units of food. He'd worked out exactly how much food we needed to live on each day. One unit of food equalled one day of travelling for each rat. With food, we could travel. Without it we would be dead. It was all very simple in a way. Then he'd worked out what weight a rat could drag over the ice and snow. He reckoned one rat could haul a bag with eighteen units of food, which gave nearly three weeks of travel at a pinch. But of course that meant half the time only exploring, the rest returning. We had to get back!

The Advance Parties had dragged a good supply of food to the First Depot. We were each dragging a full load of food from the ship, and by the time we'd eaten our daily allowance we would still have plenty to spare when we reached the Depot. The Commander reckoned that we had enough food units for our expedition to last six weeks, which would certainly, he said, be enough to reach the South Pole and get back home. It seemed to me to be a very long time to be out on the Great Ice Plain. But The Commander was full of confidence. His confidence rubbed into me like yeast into flour. We'd get there! We would succeed. We were ships' rats. There was nothing a ships' rat couldn't do.

The first week's travel was hard but we were fit, after our exercise regime. The sun rolled around the sky almost all hours in the twenty-four now. We thought travelling at night would be safer in the beginning as a precaution against skuas or any other dangers, although we didn't fear finding any local humans where we were going. During the day we slept curled up in hollows in the snow, after burying our food bags.

On the fourth day a blizzard raced in, driving fine snow over the ground so we couldn't see our way. We stayed inside our snow holes, reasonably warm. We got terribly hungry during the blizzard. We chewed snow, and learned a lesson. From now on each of us dug a hole big enough to sleep in with our food bag. The lost time was made up by a forced march. The only problem was our appetites. This kind of work made us ravenously hungry and we couldn't wait for each meal! Lovely grub! The difficulty was we could have eaten twice as much.

The First Depot was easy to find, hidden under a mound of snow beyond the end of a narrow bluff, just as the Advance Parties had described. But when we loaded all the waiting food units into our bags we could not budge them. The Commander drummed his claws in anger. We *had* to take all the food with us. The only way was to relay the stuff.

What a tedious, tiring job that was. We marched for half the night, left The Commander to guard what we had carried, then Eddie and I ran back to the Depot, picked up the rest, and dragged it to The Commander, dead tired with three journeys instead of one. We found the way by following our tracks in the snow.

Next evening after our sleep we got ready to do the same thing. Leave some of the food units behind, drag what we could for about five hours, then I would guard it while The Commander and Eddie went back and relayed the rest.

The empty white surface we walked across carried the imprint of all that touched it. Sometimes the surface was glassy hard and we slipped, leaving tiny scratch marks. Sometimes it was like baked earth and we moved over the surface with barely a record of our passing. Sometimes we sank into fine snow which left clear footprints. But our heavy food bags made long drag marks. The wind continually blew the fine snow along the surface of this Great Ice Plain, and the drag marks stayed, raised and clear, like a reversed print.

For five nights we relayed, The Commander fuming at the delays, each of us irritated and tired by the deadly repeated journeys, the endless leapfrogging. At the beginning of the sixth day The Commander announced a new plan. We were to make a Second Depot leaving exactly the number of food units we needed to get back to the First Depot on our return. 'We can carry the rest,' said The Commander. 'It's much more than the weight we are used to, but every day we eat a little of it, and that reduces the weight.'

He laughed, but it was a small grim laugh. It was strange to be carrying everything that we depended on, to know that nowhere could we find anything to help us in need, to save us from starvation.

We stood in the great white emptiness, with the sun casting peculiar rings and shafts of light in the sky. Crystals of ice fell like glittering dust through the air. The silence was absolute. Eerie. Oppressive. Not one living thing could be seen, apart from us, or even imagined.

We piled up a mound of snow as high as we could, with our precious food units inside. We had nothing to mark our little mound to help us find it again. Not even a stick! What a joke. Nothing grew here. I felt very fearful. Would the tracks we made on the endlessly similar surface be enough to lead us back to this small heap of snow, this tiny spot like a white anthill in a white desert? But I said nothing. It wouldn't do. I didn't even discuss my thoughts with Eddie. We all had to stay confident,

support each other, not criticise, or doubt.

But, privately, I gazed around searching for some way to find this Second Depot again. Far in the northern distance, in the direction we had come from, I could just see the top of the great volcano poking above the horizon, with the top of its neighbour mountain. I stared and stared at the reminder of our home in this Unknown Land, pushing the image hard into my memory. Our lives could depend on it.

We had been out thirteen days. With each step we were treading where no rat had ever trod. We were pioneers. We gripped the heavy food bags and bent our bodies to the task of dragging.

Drag drag, drive drive, from the moment we got up till it was time to turn in. The bags were desperately heavy. Our muscles ached. Sometimes the Great Ice Plain was all hollows and ridges like the solid swell of a frozen ocean, and we lost sight of what lay ahead as we went into each white hollow. Sometimes it was covered in ripples as if the wind was blowing over the surface of a lake. Except the ripples had frozen, and their edges were sharp, which hurt our feet. Sometimes the surface was easy to walk on. But sometimes we trudged through soft fine snow, like sand, jerking the weights of our food bags, sweating in our thick fur coats, because it was warm now in the sun.

Wherever we looked there was the same white horizon in all directions. Next day, at the end of the hard work of hauling, there was the endless whiteness again, the same white horizon surrounding us like a circle. It was difficult to believe that we were getting anywhere.

The sun shone out of an intensely blue sky. Ice crystals, falling as if from nowhere, rested on the snowy surface as light as thistledown. They glittered rainbow-coloured like a carpet of jewels. Then a little breeze would begin and pick up the fine ice crystals, rattling them against our legs, pricking at our skin like tiny needles.

The dazzling glare from the snow hurt our eyes so much we had to travel at night again. Even then the sun which never now sank below the horizon glinted and glared into our eyes. Each of us suffered attacks of snow blindness, when we saw double, and our eyes felt filled with burning sand, then wept, and leaked, and we could not see. There was nothing for it but to creep into a snow hole and rest.

One afternoon we woke to a frightening world where all the rules had suddenly changed. We took three steps and fell over. Another three, and we stepped into space, without seeing the gap beneath our feet. More steps, and we bumped into unseen snow-drifts. Yet there was light

– an even kind of glary whitey light. We had seen this light before. It gave no shadows. The horizon disappeared and there was no difference between snow and sky. Everything was the same. It was as if we were crawling around inside a bowl, and we didn't know what was up, what down, where edges were, even if there were any. It was horrible. We struggled on, tumbling, stumbling, as if we were blind, yet we *could* see. But what we saw didn't work. We had to stop, and sit it out, and waste precious time.

The Commander's brain went on like a machine, calculating days, distances, food units. At least as we ate our daily rations our bags became lighter to drag.

Eddie and I knew that each of us was worrying about exactly where the South Pole was. We'd discussed it endlessly before we left. Of course we couldn't ask The Commander. He seemed to know what he was doing. We had been travelling for two and a half weeks. After three weeks we were meant to be turning for home. But we didn't seem to be getting anywhere different. It was all more of the same thing, travelling over an endless relentless vast frozen plain.

On the nineteenth day of exploring, The Commander decided to reduce our food rations. We were hungry enough, pully-hauly every night, as Eddie called it, trudging along over the Ice Plain. But The Commander said that we needed to do more days travelling than he had thought. We had to make up for missed days, like the time lost relaying, or when we had to stop for blizzards, or the weird white light when we fell over. So instead of three food units a day between three of us, we would have to manage on two.

So the time of hunger began. And so began our real troubles. The travelling had been terribly hard. Now our muscles ached more than ever. Our skin was cracked and blistered with the cold and glare. We found that we damaged more easily – we mended more slowly – we were showing real signs of wear and tear. We couldn't pull as hard or for so long. Food gave us energy, but we weren't getting enough food. It was pretty basic stuff, ground meat mixed with fat, hard biscuits, a little butter, oatmeal, dried bacon. Much of it was frozen solid. But we all found ourselves watching the others, jealous, sure someone was getting more than their fair share. My mind kept on saying 'greedy blighters, greedy blighters,' like a chant. I knew it was because my stomach gnawed with hunger, but I couldn't stop the words in my head.

So I invented a kind of game for sharing food called Fair Shares. One of us took the food for the day and divided it as best as he could into three equal portions. Then, if it was my turn, I shut my eyes, while Eddie or The Commander pointed to a portion of food and called out, 'Whose is this?' I couldn't see which one they pointed at and called out a name. It was a simple method and it worked, so that ended the jealousy. But not the pain of hunger.

At the end of the third week, after we had licked up every last crumb of our meagre meal, The Commander told us the plans. We would soon make a new depot, he said, Depot Three, and hide enough food there – at reduced rations of course – to take us back to the Second Depot. We would still have twenty food units left after building Depot Three, enough to make a dash for the South Pole. The Commander said that we should get there in just under a week, which was stretching our food to the limit, but we wouldn't be wasting energy because now we didn't have so much to drag as before.

All day when I should have been sleeping I worried about the new Depot. I wanted desperately to get to the South Pole. What was the point of all this effort if we didn't get there? But how in all this terrible unending whiteness would we find our tiny Depot on the way back? All sign of our home mountains had long gone. There were no landmarks at all. We ships' rats have a good sense of direction. Our Commander was using shadows, the position of the sun, all the things we know about. But this was asking too much.

I pushed out of my snow hole and paced about. It was a perfect summer day. The bluest sky. The most sparkling snow. The clearest air. So beautiful I forgot my troubles. I gazed at the enormous expanse of snow desert. Then I saw something that I swear had not been there yesterday. On the distant horizon, to the right of our line of travel, I distinctly saw a mountain. A wonderful snow-covered mountain, just rearing its head above the horizon. I shouted for the others. We all stared in disbelief.

And together we said, 'The South Pole.'

Eddie had hidden a piece of chocolate in his bag as a special treat saved for a special celebration. Now he brought it out and we nibbled the iron-hard square, slowly, savouring every tiny morsel, till there was nothing left. That night we set off with willing hearts towards the mountain. 'Ho for the Pole,' we sang as we marched along. Our voices sounded very thin in that great vastness.

A day later we made our Third Depot. But now with the view of our mountain to help us we had at least a good chance of finding it again.

We marched towards the mountain, our light bags bumping behind us. Yet their lightness was a threat, because this was it. We had no more food when they were empty.

Strangely the mountain hardly got closer. It was as if that first view had been a mirage, to beckon us on. The Pole was being hard to get.

And we were so desperately hungry. When we slept we dreamed of food, always food. And always we never ate it. I dreamed of roast beef, all dripping juices and glorious fat, and it would be whisked away just as I climbed on the plate. Eddie dreamed of afternoon teas, enormous wonderful afternoon teas, with rich fruit cakes, and ham sandwiches, and cream cakes, and chocolate cakes with chocolate icing, and scones with strawberry jam and cream. He would run up the table leg into all this food, then the table would be tipped up, and everything spilt, and he would get nothing. And The Commander. He dreamed of being in a baker's shop with fresh crusty bread, and rich meat pies, and sausage rolls. But sometimes he actually dreamed that he ate the food, and Eddie and I couldn't bear to hear about his delicious dream meals.

Hunger made us feel the cold. Hunger made us weary. Hunger was making us ill and weak, aching in every joint, chests hurting. Still we plodded on, and the mountain got nearer, and the days crept by, and our food bags got lighter.

The surface of the Great Ice Plain began changing. It became rougher, more crumpled, as if it was being squeezed. Then Eddie fell down a crevasse. Not deep, and he was able to scramble out, but it gave us a terrible shock. Danger was everywhere in this Land. It happened before a word could be uttered. I was next, but it wasn't me that broke through the bridge of snow hiding the crevasse, but my bag. The weight of the bag began dragging me back, back towards the lip of the crack. I shouted out, and The Commander turned around and saw me just in time, and grabbed my arm and held firm.

We struggled on uncertainly over an ever more contorted surface, blocks of ice rearing up, wide yawning cracks – crevasses with their coats off, I called them. At least we could see they were there.

The Commander's eye glittered. He kept urging us on, on towards the mountain. We weren't going to be defeated. We were a brave and dogged band. We were giving it all we had. We were fighters and we'd keep fighting. Difficulties were just there to be overcome.

But underneath. Underneath we were frightened. We knew well that if we went too far we would never be able to get back. We had been out many more days than

124

planned. We had been on reduced rations for so long. We were weak. We *had* to turn with enough food to return. That was the terrible decision. And it had to be made. Before it was too late.

What if we did reach the South Pole? If we couldn't get back, no one would know what we had done. Or if we died here amongst the crevasses without ever reaching the South Pole, no one would know what we had done. Our journey would have been in vain. All the effort would have been pointless. We would be unknown heroes. I didn't want to die like that. Nor did Eddie. Life is short enough. We were not so sure about The Commander. He was courageous, determined, proud, and driven. He was a rat with an obsession.

Then the weather closed in. We dared not move amongst such crevassed ice. We lay in our snow holes not eating, because we had not a spare crumb. We sucked snow, and the liquid gave us some comfort. But terrible hunger gnawed at our stomachs. We were thin. Our fur coats hung loose about us.

This had to be the end of our journey. We could not go on. But next day The Commander said, 'We will make one last march towards the mountain. Then we will turn.'

I knew that The Commander had to do it. We had failed. But he had to feel he had done his utmost, pushed at the very edges of the possible.

We marched doggedly towards the mountain. The surface of the ice worsened. Cracks gaped, big enough to swallow a whaleboat. Tumbled blocks of ice littered their floors. The ice seemed to groan, and sometimes there were sharp bangs, like explosions.

We could see the bare rock precipices of the mountain where the snow could not stick, and its great white snowfields. The wind blew a plume of snow from its peak, and glaciers hung at the heads of its valleys. There was a distant roar and blocks of snow tumbled and slid from an overhanging lip, pieces rolling and bouncing down the slopes, snow smoke rising from the fall.

But now we could also see more mountains. Mountains beyond this mountain. And the doubt came. If there were more mountains, could this really be the South Pole? Why not another mountain? A terrible thought to poison the mind.

We stopped. The Commander stared at the mountains. His fists were gripped tight. His shoulders were hunched. He stared, and stared. Then he turned away. Without a word we began the long march back.

TWENTY–FOUR

Our food bags bumped along behind, ominously light. 'We can move faster now,' said Eddie, trying to be cheerful. 'We won't take as long to get back to our Depot as we did to get here.' Not to have reached the South Pole was a terrible blow. But we were both desperately happy to have turned. Still The Commander said nothing.

First we had to get through the crevassed area. We slithered and skidded, caution thrown aside in our hurry. Somehow we got through with no accidents, though several times one of us began slipping into a crevasse. We saved ourselves by throwing the body forward and scrabbling desperately at the edge.

Then we were back on the wide open surface of the Great Ice Plain again. Lonely insects on that enormity, under the empty huge sky. Our tracks were visible, thanks be, tiny scratches in a waste of ice and snow. We needed to travel when we could see them clearly which meant more daylight travel, and more sunglare, and aching painfilled eyes. One day was ridiculously hot, and we lay, panting. Here! In the land of ice and snow!

Then we had two days of food left only, not another shred to eat. And a bad light day happened. The Commander wanted to travel. I worried that we would lose our way in the glaring white light. Eddie worried that one of us might break a leg as we stumbled over unseen drifts and ridges. That was a disaster too awful to contemplate. In these desperate circumstances we said what we thought. The Commander gave in and we coiled down into snow holes. We were all chewing at our bags now, for comfort, and the memory of food they held, except we had to restrain ourselves, because the bags were our lifeline, we had to keep them whole. The draw cords were even more difficult to resist. I could have eaten mine a hundred times over. I sucked them instead. We were simply ravenous.

Lying in my snow hole I got out my most precious possession which I had looked at so often on this trip, my piece of moss. I held it, and smelt it, and put it to my skin. I loved it, this reminder of home. Then, with a deep sigh, I divided it up equally into three tiny pieces. We played Fair Shares. And each of us ate my moss, making it last hours and hours in the mouth.

I felt a bit better afterwards. Perhaps my lucky moss *had* brought luck. Whatever, when the light cleared, and the strange whiteness went, we set off with a little more strength.

We drove ourselves forward, limping, weak, stopping to rest, all the time watching anxiously for the signs which would lead us to the tiny mound of snow which hid our precious food. Depot Three – how we longed for it! Checking back for the view of the mountain, looking forward, watching the frail signs of our outward passage. Fear and hunger drove us on. The sour gnawing of hunger. The fear of dying in this dreadful place. We did not grumble or complain. That wasn't what was done. But inside. Inside was the leaden lump of fear.

Then, with unspeakable gratitude, and the deepest relief, we found our Depot. We dug down and there was our food. But how much we wanted to fall on it, eat too much, take more than our share, gobble and gorge it! We had to exercise the most disciplined self-control. We knew that those exactly calculated food units were our life line. And we knew that they had already been reduced, that they were much less than full allowance. But we had been on part rations for so long we hardly knew how to manage.

We ate our portion, then slept, then moved straight on; there was no spare food for us to wait and rest our weary bodies. The food dreams visited us at every sleep now. As we walked, I thought of food, and talked of food. I made lists of food. I went over every detail of past meals. I planned every mouthful of future feasts. I couldn't get the subject out of my head. I will never, never refuse a meal ever again to a starving rat, I thought. Never.

We counted every footstep of every day of the ten days between Depot Three and the Second Depot. We had been on the march now for five weeks. Three days out from the Depot a blizzard struck. Big soft snowflakes fell. The air was almost warm. Although we had suffered from the cold, it was always a dry cold. Now, inexplicably, this snow was wet, and we shivered miserably in our damp fur. Our food bags became sodden.

We had no spare food at all. No margin for anything. We should have been prepared. There was no reason why there shouldn't be blizzards. I suppose we'd been lucky with the weather. We lay in our snow holes listening to the whine and roar of the wind and wretchedly wasted a day we could not spare, each nibbling one quarter of a biscuit we could not spare. The bad times struck harder than ever. But now we were much weaker, much less able to manage. Doing even a small job was difficult, and took three times longer than it should.

We staggered up after the blizzard. The going was difficult. We sank into the soft new snow, so each step was more effort, and took longer. Dragging our bags was an exhausting struggle. Worst of all the new snow hid our outward tracks.

Two days away from the Second Depot Eddie collapsed. I was leading, because we took it in turns. 'I have to sleep,' he said, 'just for a minute,' and he fell in his tracks. In a moment he was sound asleep. We kicked him to try and make him stir. But he would not wake.

The Commander sank down, grim-faced. We were each of us at the very edges of our endurance, on the borders of surviving. I felt myself swaying, light-headed, falling sideways. Yet – I don't know where it came from – but I felt a grim determined strength that we must all get back. We must not die here. Not here, in this forsaken place. Not here, at the end of the world. The Commander is one of the toughest rats. But his eyes were sunk in his head with the exhaustion of leadership. Together we made a bed for Eddie from our two bags and dragged him along, a terrible weight, but we did it.

When we stopped, we reckoned we were only a long day's travelling from the Second Depot. I knew where it should be. The picture of the two mountains was etched in my brain. I agreed with The Commander that he should stay with Eddie, who could no longer walk. I would go on alone to the Second Depot and bring back food.

I left them both, and with a kind of unnatural energy stumbled and ran, like a rat demented, and walked and crawled, then ran again, with my nose to the ground, almost scenting the track, till at long last I reached the spot. There were our two mountains just poking over the horizon, the first sight of the familiar world, of home. I fell on my knees with gratitude, and weakness.

Our food was safe. I ate, and rested, then put food in the bag, some special rations I knew we had, chocolate and a little cheese, special food for special needs, and took it back. Eddie was a little better after his rest. We ate, and came on very slowly to the Depot.

Now we had only a six-day journey back to the First Depot. But we had a deep, nagging worry. We had left no food at all at this Depot. The Commander had ordered a party to bring some food units out to it from the ship. But what if something had gone wrong? What if they had never got there? We would be so close to home, yet we would starve. We had no crumb of spare food. And we did not have the strength to sustain any kind of blow. We were totally done up, all three of us.

It was difficult to tell who was weaker. We were dirty, thin, weather-beaten, frostbitten, unrecognisable. Our lips were raw, our noses and ears peeling and sore. Our joints ached, our bones creaked, our eyes were bloodshot, our feet were cut, our fingers and tails were swollen. Our fur was dull, ragged. We shook when we were cold, uncontrollably. We coughed, and our chests hurt. Our teeth felt loose in our heads. We felt old, and tired, and our stomachs ached continually.

Yet we kept up the dull plod, plod, dragging our bags which were pathetically light. At least we could travel again at night, because we knew the way home. But now the cold began to get to us and we suffered miserably. We felt the fatal numbness creeping into our toes and fingers and had to stop, and stop again, to rub our skin back to life.

We approached the First Depot. Apprehensive. Fearful. Then The Commander yelled excitedly. There were new footprints around the snow mound. So there would be food.

Our mates on the ship had brought out a few special treats with the food units, sardines, prunes, chocolate. We fell on the wonderful comforting stuff. There was enough for us to rest one full day. We lay around, happy, exhausted, light-headed with relief. Then, loading our bags for the last time, we set out on the final stage. Foolishly relaxed. We had been alone on the inland ice for so long we had forgotten to watch for other living things. Plodding along, The Commander suddenly looked up. 'Flatten,' he hissed. 'Dig yourselves in! It's the local humans!' In the distance we could see shapes coming towards us, two-legged, humans definitely. We dug down into the snow, dragging our bags under, leaving just space for our eyes to peer out.

Slowly the local humans came towards us. Here in the New Land distances can be so tricky, and things look closer than they are. We waited, and waited, hearts beating loudly. At last they were near. At last we were seeing them. Would they be fierce? Covered in hair? Suddenly – 'They're our Hefties!' said The Commander disgustedly. A small party of Hefties shuffled by, dragging two sledges behind them.

After this we took much greater care. Gradually, familiar landmarks came into view. We were wearier than imagining. But so glad to be nearly home. We hoped that someone would be watching out for us, and come to meet us. But no one was.

So, late one night, we came round the headland and

saw to our infinite relief the ship in the ice just as we had left it. We climbed on board by ourselves. A small party, returned from the inland ice. We had not reached the South Pole. But we had striven and endured as best we could. And we had been the furthest south. By a long, long way.

TWENTY-FIVE

We had so much to tell! So much to hear! But first we wanted food and rest. We slept, and ate and ate, and slept, then ate some more. Our friends watched astonished as we stuffed down enormous meals. They listened patiently as we told every detail of our Southern Journey, over and over. It was an effort to move so we lolled about. Gradually our stomachs began to feel normal, our bones and joints stopped aching, and we began to look like ourselves.

The first important thing for us to find out about was the ship. It was still frozen into the ice, gripped tight. This was a surprise. After all, we had sailed into our little bay a year ago, so why shouldn't we be able to sail out of it now? But ice still held the sea in thrall, all the way out to the place where we had found open water in spring.

The second important thing was the news of our friends. Many expeditions had been carried out by our brave Volunteers. No one had come to real harm. But exciting stories of adventures, near misses, and amazing sights filled the hours as we sat around eating, and talking, and resting our bodies.

The third important thing were the results. No local humans had been found. No bears or wolves. No trees or bushes anywhere, no fruit or seeds. There was some lichen clinging to rocks. A scrap of moss. The odd tiny minuscule plant, like a memory of other plants.

No place at all, anywhere, had been found where we could build safe homes for the winter.

The conclusions were horribly clear. We ships' rats *could* live here in the summer along the edges of the land. Surviving wouldn't be easy, because we could only really rely for food on penguin chicks and eggs, birds and their eggs, and any dead animal, and we would have to compete with the thieving skuas. Not to mention a huge bird with a beak like a shovel that ate anything dead, and living things as well. Inland was impossible for us. The Southern Expedition had shown that.

But in winter? There was nothing. No food. We could save and bury some summer supplies. But we reckoned that we could not live permanently in this Unknown Land unless we lived with humans. We ships' rats can normally live without humans. We don't have to have their buildings, their towns, their barns and ports. But here – we had a problem. We could live with Hefties as long as they stayed in their ships. But we reckoned that we could not live permanently on land. Pedro had done it, for one winter. Possibly some of us could have survived life in the big hut, if the Hefties had moved in. But we would always be temporary, travellers. Visitors.

The Unknown Land would not do for us ships' rats. Nor for any rat. We could not live here. We would not live here.

It was a relief to have come to a decision. There would be no Stayers. We were all Leavers. Our band of Volunteers would not be divided.

So now it was just a question of waiting for our ship to depart.

The Hefties were doing all the right things. They were down in the engine room checking the engine and boilers. They had dug the whaleboats out of the ice, and hooked them back on board. Everything was ready. Except open water!

Fergal and I were sitting one evening on top of the barrel lashed to the mainmast, talking about our summer adventures, when Fergal suddenly stopped, and stiffened. 'I've been here too long,' he mumbled. 'I'm seeing things.' And he pointed.

Away in the distance, to the north, just poking above a line of hills, were *the masts of a ship*.

TWENTY–SIX

We could not believe it. We had lived so long in these uninhabited wilds, so far from civilisation, the sight of something from the outside world filled us with profound emotion. My heart lurched. The masts could not be true. Yet I wanted them to be, so badly. Suddenly the rest of the world flooded back. What had been happening? Where was the ship from? Would there be ships' rats on board, bringing news for us? What had happened to my Clemmy? Was she all right? What about my family? I was desperate to know.

Fergal and I almost tumbled down on to the deck and raced to spread the news. Within minutes rats were swarming up the mast, clambering over the barrel, standing tiptoe, streaming along the spars, peering into the distance. It was true. There definitely was a ship.

We were sure that the Hefties didn't know yet. There were only a few on board. Most were off on their own expeditions.

The Commander called an instant Briefing. He could hardly get silence.

'Scouts will check as soon as possible the details of the ship.' He smiled. 'We must hope that she brings some of our companions, and news from home.'

We could not wait. We kept shinning up the mast to see if the ship was any closer. The masts hardly seemed to move. 'It's the dratted ice,' said The Pilot. 'We can't get out, and that ship can't get in.'

The Hefties knew now. Their flag waved from the flag-pole, and it hadn't done that before.

Our Scouts came back without any news. They hadn't taken enough supplies to reach the ship. The ship was further away than it looked. The usual problem in this Unknown Land. You couldn't trust your eyes about anything. Nothing was as it seemed.

But before the Scouts could set out again a wonderful thing happened. We heard a great Hefty cheering. Sledges drew up at the side of our ship piled with packages and bags, pulled by happy Hefties. 'There's some strange faces there,' said Pedro, who was good at Hefty faces. 'They *must* be off the new ship.'

We watched as the sledges were unloaded, and bulky sacks, boxes, all kinds of packages lifted up on deck. Hefties started carrying the stuff down below.

Suddenly we saw rats. Two of them. Complete strangers. Sleek, healthy, cheeky looking ships' rats. They came creeping out of one of the bags, bold as brass, then slipped behind some ropes. The Pilot was down on deck like a flash. The Commander ordered us into the Meeting Place.

We stood there, a scruffy-looking lot of weathered thick-coated frost-hardened rats, welded together by our shared experience. We were the Winterers. Suddenly we felt shy. It would be difficult to talk to strangers, to look them in the eye. We had seen no new faces in over a year.

The Pilot came in with the two rats. 'Meet Jose and Gerald,' he said. 'Scouts off the new ship.'

'Talk to us,' said The Commander.

And so we listened. And the news of the outside world came into our little world. We heard how the new ship had been docked at our Dock, our own Dock, by our river, exactly a year after our ship. How our Leader Blackwall and his Seniors had observed everything going on board, and come to the decision that the new ship, although very small, might be headed for the Unknown Land. How a tight little group of new Volunteers had been chosen. How we were missed by our friends and families, how news of us was longed for and our fate discussed, night after night. How the new band of Volunteers had joined their ship, and watched, and hoped; till finally their ship did turn south, after the last port, and meet the ice. How they had battled storms, and icebergs, and pushed through the frozen sea. How they had reached land where their Hefties found some old

Hefty huts – Pedro's face lit up. But they hadn't found us. How their Hefties had finally landed at the shelving beach where our Hefties had left the wooden post propped up among the hordes of penguins. Then how their ship had battled through thick ice, barely moving, till it had rounded a headland, sailed past the great volcano, and stopped when it could go no further, blocked by the frozen sea. And how – at last – with intense relief and excitement, they had seen the masts of our ship poking above the hills to the south, and known that they had found us, and that their journey had not been in vain.

We sat in silence, marvelling at the chance that had brought our friends on such a perilous journey, to meet us here in the great Unknown Land. Then we leaped up, gave three cheers, sang the Ships' Rat Song rousingly, and clustered round Jose and Gerald begging for news. And dear fellows, they had news for each of us, and special messages. And Eddie and I knew that Vanilla and Clemmy were all right, and still loved us. We were blissfully happy. All was well with the world.

Then, needless to say, we celebrated, down there in the hold, with a mother of all parties. Billy Stumps and The Tickler roared out songs, and we danced and drank till we dropped. The Commander, Eddie and I hadn't really wanted to celebrate when we got back from the Southern Journey. Now we made up for it.

TWENTY–SEVEN

We waited for the new ship to reach us. But still it didn't. Our Scouts reported that the ice was slowly breaking up. Sluggishly, in small bits. Why didn't the ice go? It wasn't here this time last year. Then the sea was open, our path free to the north. This year we were trapped.

One good thing. The packages brought on the Hefty sledges included some fresh food. We got in amongst the potatoes, nibbling their creamy crispness. And the cheese! Real cheese, crumbly, smelling of farms and clean dairies. We gorged on the yellow treasure. We'd been eating powdered cheese for too long, food fit for Hefties, not rats. Then Kettles found an apple. We'd almost forgotten what an apple looked like. We all gathered round gazing at the red and green streaked skin, smelling the delicious sharp fresh smell. Kettles let each of us have one bite. And so we shared it.

Some of us showed Jose and Gerald around. They wanted to see everything. They couldn't manage the ice and snow particularly well. We realised how much we'd learned in our year. They were keen to stay with us, so two Scouts, Lasher and Biter, hitched a ride in an empty sledge to their ship, to report our news.

All our Hefties came back from their expeditions. At least they came back without the dogs they'd taken. Good riddance. Pedro said the Hefties might have eaten the dogs. But most of us reckoned our Hefties wouldn't do that. They probably died of exhaustion, or more likely ran away.

What with the new Hefties from the new ship, and our Hefties back again, the place was very crowded. We had to be extremely careful not to be seen. We didn't want to spoil our record by being careless, not at this late stage!

The darkness of night was beginning to creep back into the days again. The year was turning. Autumn was coming. The chill of winter echoed in our souls. The sun rarely shone now. Instead there were grey overcast skies and the return of the biting cold east wind. We wanted to get going. It was more than time to leave.

We all felt uneasy. Hefty sledges arrived from the new ship every day piled high with supplies which were loaded into our holds. Our Scouts reported that the new ship was creeping closer. More ice had broken away. But there was still a solid barrier of thick white ice between us and freedom. We didn't really care about the new ship. It was our ship that mattered. We were still trapped.

Eddie and I, with Fergal, Skelly and Padders – we decided we had to do something. Waiting was getting on our nerves. We requested permission from The Commander to visit the new ship.

We bustled round collecting a few stores for our trip. We didn't want to travel with the Hefties on their sledges. Dangerous work, for Scouts only. No, we wanted, I suppose, one last brief expedition, one last feel of the bag of supplies dragging behind, the draw cords gripped in the teeth, stepping out across the ice, the lure of the open road. It wasn't far. We'd probably find food to eat on the way, a few eggs, a chick. To avoid any risk of running into travelling Hefties we planned not to go straight out across the sea ice but to take a more roundabout route along the shore.

Over the hills, past the high straight-sided rock which stuck up a bit like a castle. Our feet sank into the snow and we were happy to be doing something. We went to sleep early. Next day it was on, on, around pock-marked boulders, over sheets of scalloped ice and stretches of sharp grit and deep drifts.

We planned to strike out across the sea ice to the ship very early in the morning before any Hefties were up. There was some difficult ice to negotiate along the ice crack where the sea ice pushed against the land, all heaved up, and broken, like tumbled blocks. Then we were out on to the ice, hauling for the ship which we could plainly see, tied up to the distant ice edge. We could sense the open ocean beyond.

I felt it first. A kind of swaying. The ice we were walking on began moving. Without any warning, the ice under our feet was beginning to shift. It heaved, slowly. There was no wind. No storm. But we could feel the swell of the great ocean working beneath us, cracking the solid ice apart.

Horrified, we started running back the way we had come. It was as if the solid surface of the Earth had suddenly started splitting and breaking into pieces. Beyond us at the ice edge the pieces began to move, carried by some unseen force, setting out on their own courses across the sea, unstoppable. Grinding, splitting sounds filled our terrified ears. Suddenly with a dreadful hissing two huge horrible heads rose up amongst the ice pieces and stared around. Black and white monstrous heads, just like Eddie and I and Fergal had seen, all that time ago, on our first expedition. Except now we knew they were killer whales.

We ran, sobbing for breath, as the ice beneath us heaved, jumping for our lives across widening strips of water, scrambling across floes, wet, waist deep in soft snow, sliding on slippery slopes, but getting closer all the time to the shore, and safety.

With an almighty boom and smash the killer whales forced their heads up through the cracked ice, splitting it into fragments. Still we ran, while around us the once silent white world broke up and crashed apart into heaving, violent motion.

With the ice beneath me sinking and rising, with a final frenzied leap, I caught the edge of the shore and shivering, shaking, threw myself down. Only now could I look for my companions. Eddie was close behind. Skelly had to swim the last bit. Fergal made the shore further down.

But there was no Padders. We raced along the shore, calling and calling. Then we saw him desperately trying to get off a floe that was moving by itself, fast, like a ship alone. Skelly climbed up a rock and saw the floe heading for a tongue of ice that stuck out into the sea. We all ran for the ice tongue. 'Jump for it when I tell you,' Skelly shouted. Padders crouched at the edge of his floe, every muscle in his strong body tensed. Just as the floe brushed the edge of the ice Skelly yelled, 'Jump,' and in a split second Padders was scrabbling up the side of the slippery ice. Safe.

We were a very subdued band that made our way back to the ship. 'Ice is dangerous,' Pedro had warned us when we first entered these seas. 'Never trust it.' Now we'd seen for ourselves how quickly ice could break apart, crash together, stay, go. We'd made our little plans. But they were nothing compared to the huge forces which directed everything in this Land.

At least the ice breaking up means that our ship will soon be free, said The Commander, when we reported back to him.

But it wasn't.

TWENTY–EIGHT

This last breakout of ice, the one that nearly finished us, brought the new ship much closer. A band of solid ice still remained. It could go at any time without warning, as we now understood. But worrying news came from the new ship where we always had Scouts stationed. A layer of thin ice had begun forming over the sea at night. It went in the morning. The season was changing fast; winter was on its way. The new ship risked being frozen in just like we had been.

The thought was too terrible to contemplate.

We huddled in corners talking, talking, rumours as always speeding round. The Commander kept to himself in his quarters.

The Pilot was quite clear what should be done. Without delay we should all abandon ship and transfer to the new ship. His words caused an outcry. Our duty was with our ice-bound ship. We ships' rats do not abandon ship unless in the direst emergency, to save ourselves. But this is what The Pilot said we would be doing. We could be trapped here for another year. We must save ourselves and leave.

Kettles said we should go. He said based on his northern experience the ice could still suddenly break out, so our ship could be released. But we rats could not risk waiting. We must move to the new ship so we were sure of getting away. We had decided to leave. So leave we must.

Pedro spoke with horror of another winter. The season would close in very rapidly, he said. We had enough supplies, and we wouldn't starve. But another long dark winter would drive some of us mad. He spoke with stark knowledge. He was the only rat who had ever spent two winters here in the New Land.

The truth was all of us wanted to get home. Home had presented itself with the new ship. It had reminded us, crowded us with memories. I couldn't wait to get back and marry my dear Clemmy. Eddie couldn't wait to see his dear Vanilla. And now he had three little ones to see, his own children, Billy, Myrtle and Ernest. Fergal was desperate to find his new love again. Every one of us had a reason to be home, someone waiting, loved ones missing him.

Early one evening just after dinner The Commander

summoned us to a Briefing. We all gathered in solemn and anxious mood.

'The situation is serious,' said The Commander, tapping his claws in the way Eddie and I knew. 'It seems impossible that our ship will be free. The new ship must leave this place within the next few days. It risks being frozen in. I have thought long and hard. My decision weighs heavily on me.'

We waited, tense, silent. We had been in this Meeting Place so often. It was part of our lives.

'I must order the abandoning of our ship.'

A sigh passed through the Volunteers, like the sound out on the Great Ice Plain when the brittle crust of snow cracked and sank down on the soft snow beneath. We felt chilled. To leave all that we knew, the place that had been our home, our little world. It was hard.

Each of us went, silent, to gather his things. We couldn't take much. Just small treasures, a memento from the ship, or from the land, a strangely coloured stone, a feather, or a small bleached white bone. The things you took from this Unknown Country were not physical. They were pictures for the inner eye, sounds for the soul's silence, feelings too deep to express.

Then we were ready to leave. No final party. No feast. It didn't seem right. We filed off the ship down on to the snow. The Volunteers abandoning ship.

We followed The Commander who led us a strange route. But we followed, obeying. Ships' Rats' Rules. Past the empty tins and wooden casks, the usual Hefty rubbish on the ice, up past the dog kennels to the big hut. At one

side an old snow-drift led in a steeply crusted slope nearly
to the roof. Up we climbed, on to the roof of the hut.
There, on the crest of the roof, we stopped.

Our black ship lay at peace below us, held in the
implacable grip of the ice, her masts and spars clearly
outlined against the vast sky. A few yellow lights
glowed from below decks. A smudge of smoke drifted
from the galley chimney.

We gazed around at the familiar landmarks. The two
small Hefty huts. The snow-streaked rocky ground. The
near hills. The distant hills. The sea ice, across to the far
mountains. And – to the south, the thing we all knew,
whether we could see it or not – the Great Ice Plain
leading south. The immense silence of this place beat
like a heart. The immense solitude of it. Its untouched

huge emptiness. Its untouchable, unimagined, splendid otherness.

We had been here, briefly. It did not care. But we did, deeply. We would never, could never, forget. The Unknown Land had entered our souls. It would mark us, for ever.

We thought of our two dead companions who would never return home. In silence we saluted our ship with raised clenched fists.

Then we left.

TWENTY-NINE

We travelled fast all night across the sea ice. The new ship was much closer now. We arrived at grey first light. A cold wind was blowing. We sprawled, waiting behind a snow-drift, while The Commander went aboard. We felt awkward, different, outsiders. On board life was going on, everyone knew what to do and where things were. We didn't know the ship. It didn't belong to us. We would have to fit into other rats' quarters.

The ship was certainly small. We eyed her, impressed that she had been able to brave the southern ice. But then we were aboard and being ushered to our new companions' Meeting Place. Jose and Gerald were there, making us all feel welcome. Our Scouts knew their

Scouts. Their Voyage Leader was large and jovial, called Captain Coal, appropriate given the blue-black sheen to his fur. He welcomed us and proposed a party. Things would be crowded, but that would make the party better.

And before we knew it we were being shown around the ship, choosing our nesting places, checking out the galley, being warned of the Hefty habits, shown the escape routes, the rat-runs, the Emergency Drill, the Disaster Stations, all the business of joining a new ship. She was certainly snug. But rather jolly. We would be all right.

The party was a success. Even if we'd been feeling reserved, it was impossible not to join in. This ship had good food. Best of all, it had fresh food — mutton, more of the delicious potatoes and cheese, yellow butter, apples — we realised how much we had been missing. We tucked in to the excellent grub and had extra whacks of everything. Then we gathered for the best singsong ever. Our friend Gerald knew more songs than we'd ever thought possible and soon we were thumping them out, and dancing and drinking. We treated our new friends to the Volunteers' Chorus,

> We've done it!
> We've been!
> We've come!
> We've seen!

Pause, for the count of three, then,

IT CONQUERED!

We laughed, and fell about, then coiled down wherever

there was a space and slept the sleep of the truly tired.

The Hefties were also having a party. Some of our ships' Hefties had come over the ice to join in. They made enough racket to block out ours.

Next morning was overcast and gloomy. Young ice had formed on the open water like heavy silk stretched over the surface. The swell beneath moved the ice up and down, but did not break through. A thick smoke of snow started swirling over the sea ice towards us, driven by a biting wind.

After lunch nearly all our Hefties got off and stood on the ice. A few stayed on board. Then, with no warning, the ice anchor was hauled in. Slowly the ship backed away from the ice-edge. We were leaving. As quickly as that. The Hefties shouted to each other, and cheered, our ship blew its whistle, and slowly the lonely group of black figures standing on the ice became smaller, and their cheers couldn't be heard. They waved their last waves, then turned with their sledges to trudge back to where they had come from. Soon we couldn't see them in the gloom, and the drifting snow.

We were sad. Of course we were sad. But we had already said our true goodbyes on the roof of the big hut. Now our noses were truly turned for home.

Our ship steamed through young ice which lay over the surface like a greasy elastic skin. As we passed the volcano we saluted its smoking bulk in respect. Fire and ice. Ice and fire. Memories of the glow from its red burning heart on black winter skies.

We were on our way! Where we had entered, we now made our exit. The road north was open.

THIRTY

Early in the evening Pedro came hurrying up to where we were lounging with our new mates. 'Look ahead,' he said grimly. 'Ice!' We rushed forward to see a band of smooth new ice stretching across the sea from shore to shore, like a barrier.

Our little ship pushed into the ice. But this kind of ice was different. It didn't crack up, break, move aside. It was like porridge, sticky sludge. It grasped us, held us, wouldn't let us through. Our ship's engines laboured and we didn't move. The stuff just piled up around our bow like mud around churning cart wheels.

All night and next day we tried to move. We were filled with despondency. After all that had happened, were we doomed to stay in this land? Would we be caught in the ice out here, where there was no protection, no safe harbour, no solid land to move on to? The thought was appalling. We were so close to our own comfortable ship in its snug little bay, yet so far. We were like a fly caught on sticky paper.

What if we did become trapped in the ice all winter? The Pilot said that our ship would probably be crushed and we would all drown. Anxiously we roamed the ship, hardly knowing where to put ourselves in the unfamiliar spaces. Our new mates kept out of our way.

Late in the afternoon Pedro reported a blizzard approaching from the south. We knew the signs. Thick grey clouds with tops like twisted hair rolling inexorably along the ice towards us, driving drift snow at stinging speed.

Suddenly the Hefties rushed into action. *They set all sails.* In a blizzard. When we were stuck! We tensed, expecting the call to Disaster Stations at any moment. The blizzard reached us. The wind gusted, then blew, with hard driving snow. The sails filled to their utmost. The masts bent like willows. The engines beat loudly. Yet we did not move. The wind blew fiercer, and now slowly, slowly, we crept forward, churning through the sticky ice, dragging forward with huge reluctance while every moment we expected the masts to snap, the sails to blow to shreds under the strain.

Then we started to go backwards. Despite the fierce wind filling the sails, despite the thrust of the engines, we were moving in the opposite direction. Truly in this

Land huge forces ruled, and we were as matchsticks in the water.

I felt completely helpless, worn out by the struggle going on around us. Slowly the ship began to gain slight headway again. The Hefties were working her towards an island. A narrow stretch of open water remained along the shore. Daringly our ship worked along the open water of the shore, bit by bit.

Then we were beyond – and, almost as if we were a cork that had come out of the neck of a bottle – we were into thinner ice. We were free.

We were only just in time. As we worked north past the land we had seen on our way south, we pushed every hour through new ice that lay strewn over the sea like the round leaves of a waterlily, each flat leaf rubbing and jostling its neighbour, with jumbled mush ice in between. The water was dark and grey. The skies were leaden. Gone were the intense blues and brilliant whites of this place during our southern voyage. Winter was coming. In our small ship we had just made our escape.

Eddie, Fergal, Padders and I went late one night into the fo'c'sle. On this new ship of ours it was a small space. We rummaged round, seeing what we could find, getting right down to the flooring. Suddenly – with a fierce squeal – a great brown rat leaped out from beneath us.

An enemy, here! We stared aghast. We had been away so long. We had almost forgotten about the brown rats. All unknowing we had cornered the brute. He stood facing us, with his horrible close-set little ears, small eyes glaring, tail lashing.

There was nothing for it. We had to fight. Either he died, or us. Each of us prepared for battle. It seemed hard, so close to our escape from this Land.

The brown rat was very strong. He fought hard and well. But there were four of us, Padders was our best, and we didn't fight by any rules. When he was dead we left him with Padders and Fergal guarding and raced along the rat-runs to get The Commander and Captain Coal.

Dead rats can't talk. So we couldn't know if he was a sole spy. Captain Coal was certain he hadn't joined the ship at our Dock at the start of the voyage. The usual thorough searches had been undertaken. No stops had been made until the port which had been our last port. That must have been where he slipped on board. The Commander reminded us all of our fright with the brown rats there, and the fight on the wharf. Careless talk in ports, he said.

An intensive search was made in every corner of the ship by our grim-faced shipmates. No sign of a brown rat. Our enemy must have been travelling alone.

We held a Council of War. There was to be no talking

at whatever port we landed. No fraternising with the local ships' rats. We were a chosen band. We must not speak until we had got home and reported.

But underneath there was a certain relief. Because we knew what we had to report. *No* rats could live in the Unknown Land. We would not have to fight for it with the brown rats. There was no competition for territory. Even if brown rats got there they would find out what we had found out. The Unknown Land would stay untouched, alone.

I went up on deck, forward, and stood by the wash port. I wanted to clear my head, to think. Small pieces of ice slipped past in the black water with a soft brushing sound. A mighty iceberg, like a piece of the Great Ice Plain we had toiled across, rode in the sea. Solid, solid ice. Unyieldingly hard.

We were sailing past the headland where we had first landed. Pedro's prison. I could see its outline, with the mountains rising beyond it. The outside edge of this great Land.

We had done what we had been sent to do. Nothing more needed to be done.

And yet. And yet. I could not forget the unfinished Southern Journey. We had got the furthest south, The Commander, Eddie and I. But there was further south to go, much further. I knew that. Perhaps even beyond the mountains. The South Pole had not been reached.

And now I, Hackle, knew that whatever I did, wherever I was, this Land would call to me. Always. Whether I listened or not. I'd never come back as a

Stayer. We'd proved that was impossible. But perhaps one day I would come back. As a Pole-seeker.

Yes. I was a Pole-seeker too.

I breathed in deep breaths of the pure sharp cold air, air as fresh as the first day that ever was. I stroked my excellent thick fur coat. My badge of being here.

I saluted the great Unknown Land. And went below.

HISTORICAL NOTE

Discovery, a newly-built wooden ice-breaker, sailed up the River Thames to East India Docks in June 1901. On the last day of July she departed for Antarctica. Heading south were her commander Robert Falcon Scott R.N., ten officers and scientists, and thirty-six men of other ranks. Only the young Australian physicist Louis Bernacchi had been to Antarctica, having just returned from the first expedition to spend a winter on the Antarctic continent.

Much was hoped for from this British National Antarctic Expedition. Antarctica was largely unknown. Only short sections of the coast had been seen. No one knew if Antarctica was a continent or a group of islands, if the South Pole was on land or, like the North Pole, in an ice-filled ocean.

Discovery anchored in a sheltered bay by Ross Island in McMurdo Sound. To the south stretched the vast Ice Barrier, a huge glacier edging slowly down from the distant mountains to the sea. Winter ice began forming around *Discovery's* hull, and she became locked into the ice.

The following summer a small wooden ship *Morning* arrived from London, to relieve *Discovery*. *Morning* could not break through the last ice separating *Discovery* from the open sea, and left again in March 1903. *Discovery* did not break free for another year. Much scientific work and a number of exploring trips had been undertaken by the men of the expedition.

The ships rats in this story who volunteered to come to the Unknown Land were brave and adventurous. Much of what happened to them parallels the experiences of Scott and his men. The sequence and timing of events in *The Pole-seekers* are as they actually occurred. Rats and humans discovered, suffered, and experienced this extraordinary place in separate but shared ways.

But all the rats in the story departed on the *Morning*. They had discovered what they came to find out. Ships rats could not survive here in the Unknown Land. No rats could, not even their enemies, the brown rats.

Scott, some officers, and scientists wrote accounts of the expedition, and Ernest Shackleton edited a newspaper during the long winter. Now, for the first time, we can read the adventures of the ships' rats.

The Journey of *Discovery* and the
National Antarctic Expedition 1901–4

21 March 1901, *Discovery* launched Dundee
 3 June, berthed East India Dock, London
31 July, sailed
29 November, arrived Lyttelton, New Zealand
24 December, left for the Antarctic
 8 January 1902, sighted the Antarctic mainland
 2 February, balloon launched, rises to 700 feet
 8 February, anchored at Ross Island, McMurdo Sound
 2 November, Southern Party of Scott, Shackleton and
    Dr Edward Wilson, set out
24 January 1903, *Morning* arrives at McMurdo Sound
 2 March, *Morning* departs
16 February 1904, *Discovery* finally breaks free from the
    ice
15 September, berths at East India Dock, London

RRS Discovery is now at Discovery Point in Dundee, Scotland, and can be visited as part of a museum of Antarctica.

In Antarctica the hut built by Scott's men is still standing at Hut Point, Ross Island. Today McMurdo Station, the largest United States Antarctic base, is built close to where *Discovery* was anchored in her winter quarters, as is New Zealand's Scott Base.

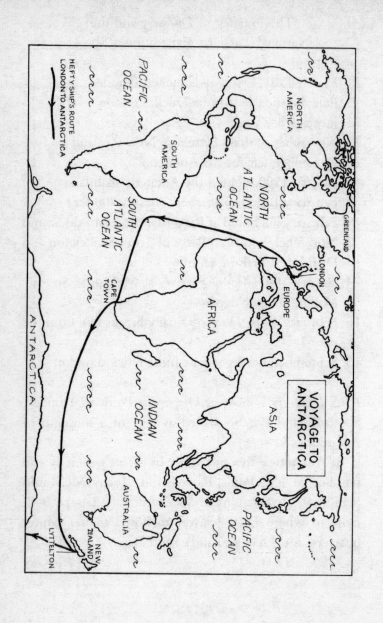

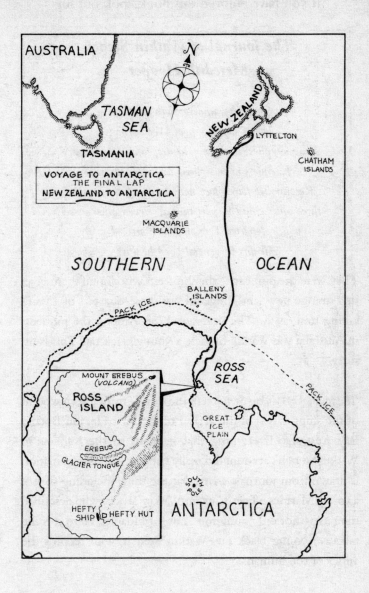

AUSTRALIA

TASMAN
SEA

TASMANIA

NEW ZEALAND

LYTTELTON

CHATHAM
ISLANDS

N

VOYAGE TO ANTARCTICA
THE FINAL LAP
NEW ZEALAND TO ANTARCTICA

MACQUARIE
ISLANDS

SOUTHERN   OCEAN

BALLENY
ISLANDS

PACK ICE

PACK ICE

ROSS
SEA

GREAT
ICE
PLAIN

MOUNT EREBUS
(VOLCANO)

ROSS
ISLAND

EREBUS
GLACIER TONGUE

HEFTY
SHIP   HEFTY HUT

SOUTH
POLE

ANTARCTICA

If you have enjoyed this book, look out for

The Journal of Watkin Stench
Meredith Hooper

Coast dry, undergrowth excellent.
Water supplies poor. Weather hot.
Food supplies: none in evidence; foraging necessary.
Enemies: none sighted. Towns, roads, nil.
Reconnoitre took place with Landing Scouts from
three other ships. Report that all eleven other vessels
which departed England have arrived safely.
All rats in general good health . . .

They were the pioneers – the ships' rats who found themselves
in a strange new land. England was three-quarters of a year's
sailing time away. The year was 1788. Among the pioneers
in Australia was Watkin Stench, a young black rat. This is his
story.

The Journal of Watkin Stench tells the story – from the viewpoint
of the ships' rats – of the arrival of the First Fleet in Botany
Bay, Australia. Everything that happens to the humans in
Watkin Stench's account did really happen. Much information
is drawn from journals written at the time, including that of
a young Marines officer, Captain Watkin Tench, who described
the rats as 'not only numerous, but formidable'. Here, it is the
talkative young black rat, Watkin Stench, who records the
antics of the humans.

A fast-moving, enjoyable story, based soundly on fact,
Watkin Stench energetically conveys the ups and downs of
the lives of the rats of the First Fleet.

WHAT PEOPLE HAVE SAID ABOUT

THE JOURNAL OF WATKIN STENCH

'I like the sight of children with their heads in a book . . . so enthralled by *The Journal of Watkin Stench* that they don't want to stop . . .'
Books for Keeps

'In his pert, lively, observant and sometimes lyrical style, Watkin records the bleakness and strangeness that faced the pioneer newcomers . . . informing, thorough and fascinating.'
Naomi Lewis in the *Times Education Supplement*

'This clever spoof history certainly deserves to be included among the host of celebratory books on early Australian history.'
Growing Point

'The journal opens with a sustained passage of suspense generated by the excitement of arrival in a strange land and never lacks that kind of interest to the end. Based on fact, it reads like the best fiction . . .'
The Junior Bookshelf